The Saturday Secret

and other stories

From Fabrian Books:
15 feel-good tales of love
and family life

by

Melinda Huber

The Saturday Secret

Author: Linda Huber https://lindahuber.net/

Author's Note and Acknowledgements

The Saturday Secret is a collection of fifteen light-hearted stories of love, friendship, and family life. All have previously been published in women's magazines, by DC Thomson & Co Ltd, Scotland, and are now released under my feel-good pen name, Melinda Huber.

I'd like to thank everyone concerned in the production of this collection, especially The Cover Collection for the (as always) amazing cover art, Yvonne Betancourt for her formatting skills, and the team at Fabrian Books for their help and encouragement. Thanks also to everyone who has supported me in real life and on social media – too many to mention, and I couldn't do without any of you!

Lastly, love and thanks to my boys, Matthias and Pascal, for their help, patience, and advice as I put this collection together.

In memory of my grandmother,
Elizabeth Raeside

Contents

The Party Partners

The invitation to Cecily's wedding came on a Saturday morning. I knew what it was straightaway, of course. Joy, my oldest sister and proud mother-of-the-bride, had talked of little else for weeks.

Still, it made me feel odd, seeing it set out in black and white like that. *Mr and Mrs Peter Maitland request the pleasure of*...

I poured myself another mug of coffee and sat staring at the invitation. All at once, I felt old. Here was Cecily, just nineteen, and already she had found the man she wanted to spend the rest of her life with. I was thirty-four with nothing but failed relationships behind me – I was beginning to feel left on the shelf. And dusty, too. Of course, I had an interesting job, loads of friends, plenty of hobbies – but still, a niggling little voice in my head was whispering that I didn't have forever to settle down and start a family...

I stood up, pushed the uncomfortable thoughts away, and started to plan what to wear on the big day.

The wedding was in the old Trinity Chapel, a charming little grey stone church standing in a mossy old churchyard. It was the perfect wedding venue; it could have been an illustration in one of the bridal magazines Joy had been devouring for the past year. I'd decided not to bring anyone – it seemed silly to invite someone just for the sake of having a male presence beside me – so I sat with my brother, Mark, and his family.

Aunt Helen and Uncle Joe were in the pew behind us. 'On your own again, Belinda?' Uncle Joe prodded my shoulder and gave me a horrible wink. 'Must be great to be young, fancy-free and–'

'Shh! Joe!' Aunt Helen hissed. 'The bride's arriving!'

I knew why she'd shushed him, though. Not because Cecily was here, but because jokes about being fancy-free just weren't funny to a thirty-four-year-old.

The ceremony was amazing, and after the obligatory church pics we all adjourned to the local Country Club for the reception and yet more photos. The photographer ushered the bridal party into the rose garden, and we posed in all the various family combinations.

When I'd done my bit, I wandered along a narrow little path between tall rhododendron bushes. I didn't want to stand around chatting to Aunt Helen and Uncle Joe, or Aunt Susan and Uncle Pat, or even my parents. I realised that for the first time, I felt awkward being alone in a group full of couples.

Maybe I should have invited Sean from work, but...

'Oh! I'm so sorry – I didn't see you!' I had walked right over two large feet clad in shiny black shoes. Their owner was perched on a low wall, gloomily clutching an empty sherry glass.

'It's quite all right,' he said gallantly, then gave me a rueful grin. 'Are you hiding too?'

I pulled a face. 'Sort of. I'm avoiding aunts with leading questions. You know the kind.'

'Don't I just. Are you Frances, by any chance?'

Frances was Joy's goddaughter; she was at least ten years younger than me. It was my turn to grin. 'Help, no. I'm Belinda Morris – the bride's aunt.'

He stood up and bowed solemnly. 'Phillip Watson – the groom's uncle. Are you alone here?'

Somehow, I found myself telling him all about how out of place I was feeling today, amongst the family pairs.

'I know, it's awful,' he said. 'They all expect you to produce a partner and offspring, and you start feeling guilty and embarrassed because you haven't. Let's pair up for the rest of the wedding, and face it out together.'

So we did. He was very attentive, and it was a relief not having to worry about who to dance with or chat to between times. Late that evening, Phillip escorted me to my car and kissed my cheek. 'It's been a lovely wedding,' he said, holding the car door open for me. 'The best for ages, thanks to you. I'll give you a call.'

I drove homewards, dreaming of Phillip's brown eyes and shy smile.

He didn't phone. I was really disappointed. We'd had fun at the wedding, and I knew I could like him a lot, given the chance. Should I call him? But then, we hadn't been on a date, had we? Circumstances had thrust us together for a few hours, that was all, and he was obviously one of those confirmed bachelors. I decided not to dream, and tried hard to follow my own advice.

Then, four weeks after Cecily's wedding, my phone rang. By this time I'd stopped expecting it to be Phillip, and I sat down suddenly when I heard his voice.

'Hi, Belinda! How's life?'

I stammered something, and inquired after his life too.

'Great, thanks. Ah – actually, I wanted to ask a favour. Are you doing anything a week on Friday?'

'I don't think so. Why?' A tiny ray of hope started to shimmer in my soul.

'My cousin's just got engaged, and they're having a big do at Chez Moi. We were such good wedding party partners, I wondered if you'd like to come with me to Trix's engagement party?'

'Of course, that would be lovely.' I beamed into my phone, but he only thanked me, told me the party details, and rang off. I was left clutching my phone, wondering if I had just made a date or concluded a business arrangement.

The engagement party was great fun. Most of the guests were in their early twenties, and Phillip and I disco-danced and shouted at each other through loud music. Personal conversation was impossible, but I enjoyed myself all the same. And maybe we could make another date now...

'Thanks, Belinda,' said Phillip, pulling up in front of my flat and switching the engine off. 'I'd have been lost in that rabble without you. Maybe we can do it again, sometime.'

He kissed my cheek. I smiled warmly and opened the car door. 'Lovely. Would you like to come in for a coffee?'

For a second he looked almost panicky. 'Oh, ah, no – thanks. Sorry. Another time, huh? I have to – I'll be in touch.'

His car zoomed up the street, and I stared after it, indignation welling up inside me. Either Phillip was incredibly shy and awkward, or he had only invited me as a convenient partner. But then – he could easily have gone to the party for ten minutes, congratulated the happy couple, and gone home again.

I shook myself. There was no point in getting worked up about it. I would be old-fashioned and leave the running up to Phillip. After his hasty retreat tonight, it would seem more than a little over-keen if *I* called *him* now.

He didn't phone.

Two weeks later, the invitation to Aunt Helen and Uncle Joe's Golden Wedding Anniversary dinner plopped onto the hall floor. I opened it and cringed. *Belinda and Partner* was written there in Aunt Helen's best calligraphy class handwriting.

I thought about it all day. I could ask Sean from work, but somehow, I just didn't want to. I could plead a previous engagement. But not many previous engagements are more important than family golden weddings. Of course, I could be ill at the last moment, but that was a bit weak, and I'd have half the family round clutching hot water bottles, anyway.

I could go alone. But that was unthinkable. Uncle Joe would have a field day.

Or, I could ask Phillip to partner me. But the way he'd rushed off after my invitation to come in for coffee… I cringed again.

In the end, I did phone him.

'Sure,' he said at once. 'One good turn deserves another. And I've really enjoyed our 'dos' haven't you?'

I ended the call feeling slightly happier. Maybe he *was* just shy. I determined to make a real effort at the golden wedding party. I had two weeks to plan some casual questions to throw into the conversation. This time, I would get to know him properly.

It wasn't easy, finding an opportunity to talk privately between dances and chats with aunts and uncles, but Phillip did open up a little at the dinner party. In a way.

'Oh, I'm hopeless with women,' he said, laughing. 'Just as well I work with animals!' (He was a vet.)

His cheerfulness unsettled me. Surely, if he really wanted to get to know me, he wouldn't sound so happy about it? And the invitation had come from me, this time. Maybe he would never have got in touch again.

'Thanks for your help tonight,' I said brightly, as I drove towards his flat.

'My pleasure. Look, ah – you can let me out here. There are never any empty spaces near my flat, um – I'll be in touch. Bye!'

This time it was my car that zoomed away.

Fortunately, I managed to get home before I burst into tears. I would never, ever go anywhere with Phillip again. It was just too humiliating. I could like him so much, if he gave me a chance – but he obviously wasn't going to. So I would forget him right now.

It was funny how many people started reminding me of Phillip. I suddenly noticed that Steve downstairs had the same glasses. Eric from the swimming club drove the same car. And my younger brother had almost the same haircut.

But every time even half a thought of Phillip came into my head, I stamped it out immediately.

A couple of weeks after the golden wedding do, my phone rang. It was Phillip.

'How are you, Belinda?'

His voice made my insides churn nervously, and I realised that my try-to-forget-him efforts had all been in vain.

'Fine,' I whispered. 'How are you?' What an idiotic start to any kind of conversation.

'Fine, fine. Belinda, I was wondering – my parents are having a little party soon, to celebrate–'

Something inside me snapped. 'No!' I yelled down the phone. 'I don't want to be your party partner. I want to be real, proper partners with someone who's interested in me as a person and not as half an invitation. I want to be cherished and sent flowers and chocolates because someone wants to make me happy, and I want to talk and laugh with someone and make them happy, and – if you don't want all that too, Phillip, then just leave me alone. This is my life, you know, not a stupid party!'

I flung my phone down on the sofa and buried my face in a cushion. Would I ever get the chance to love someone, and be loved in return? I sobbed for a solid fifteen minutes, then trailed through to the loo and rinsed my face. Bleakly, I decided to wash the bathroom floor. If I couldn't be loved, at least I could be useful.

I was standing with wet knees and wearing yellow rubber gloves, squeezing the cloth in the bucket, when the doorbell rang. Heck. I'd forgotten that Marianne, my middle sister, sometimes came round on Tuesday evenings. I dragged myself to the door.

There on the doorstep, nearly hidden behind the most enormous bunch of roses, stood Phillip. He had a huge box of chocolates under his arm, too. He thrust both flowers and chocs into my rubber-gloved hands and grabbed my shoulders.

'Belinda – I'm sorry – it's just – I didn't know if you really were interested, and I – I couldn't find the words!'

He looked absolutely wretched. For the first time in ages, hope was dancing in front of my eyes.

'Belinda. I've loved you since the moment you walked over my feet at Cecily's wedding, but I'm so hopeless at all this and oh, come here!'

He pulled me closer and kissed me. Fireworks seemed to shoot off in all directions.

After a moment, I stepped back and pulled my rubber gloves off. 'Come on. I'm winding time back to the evening of your cousin's engagement party. Would you like to come in for coffee?'

The relief on his face made me laugh. This time, there would be no zooming away...

Family Matters

'You mean your sister wants us to look after the children for six weeks while she and Bruce go off to Africa on voluntary service?' Gary stared across the kitchen table, a bemused expression on his usually humorous face.

Sharon patted his arm. It wasn't that Gary didn't like children. He was an enthusiastic uncle when they had to look after Ben and Katie, taking swing parks and baby buggies in his stride, and enjoying it, too. It was more that he didn't want children as part of his daily life – yet.

'Plenty of time for kids later on,' he'd said at the start of their marriage, and Sharon had agreed. After all, they were only twenty-three at the time. They would have ten years of independence and careers first, and then think about a baby.

Now they were halfway through the ten years and enjoying every minute. And a long visit from Ben and Katie would give them just a taste of being mums and dads.

'It'll be fun,' said Sharon firmly, cutting Gary

another slice of chocolate cake. 'And I think they should go, don't you? Bruce has been involved in this school project since the beginning, and now that it's at the starting out stage, Jill's teaching experience will be invaluable.'

Gary nodded thoughtfully. 'It'll be you doing most of the work here, love. By the time I get back in the evenings, the kids'll be going to bed.'

He dropped a kiss on the top of her head on the way to get more coffee.

Sharon walked through their bungalow that day, looking at her home with new eyes. It was spacious enough, though the kids would have to share a room. At least there was a garden, and her work as a freelance illustrator meant there would be no problems about looking after the children. She lifted an Edinburgh crystal vase and pulled a face. They would need to make the place toddler-proof; Katie was into everything these days. Sharon smiled at the thought of her niece's happy little face, and then shivered. Six weeks! Would she cope with being a mother-substitute all that time? The photo on the sideboard caught her eye – a family snap taken at Katie's christening, cheesy grins all over the place. Of course she would cope, realised Sharon, warmth rushing through her at the thought of it. As a matter of fact, she was looking forward to it.

A sunny Saturday morning in mid-May saw the arrival of Ben and Katie, with what seemed like an incredible amount of luggage. The children were used to Sharon looking after them and settled down quickly in the kitchen, Ben drawing dinosaurs and Katie running around as Sharon sliced kiwi for a 'welcome' snack.

'Look, Auntie Sharon,' said Ben proudly, waving a green and brown creation in the air. 'This is a brontosaurus. They don't have these in Africa, but they do have elephants, and dad's going to take a photo of the very first elephant he sees and email it to me. Is the computer on?'

'I think so,' said Sharon cautiously. 'My phone is, anyway. But they won't actually have left Heathrow yet, darling. I don't think they'll email you elephants for a day or two.'

Ben's face fell slightly, but he added a few more teeth to the brontosaurus, then looked at it thoughtfully. 'Auntie Sharon – why did all the dinosaurs die? They were so big and strong.'

Gary came in at that moment and ruffled the little boy's hair. 'That's the million dollar question, Benny-boy. No one really knows. You'll just have to be a famous scientist when you grow up, and find out for us all.'

'Want juice,' said Katie, stretching both arms up to Sharon. 'Where's Mummy?'

Her lips were trembling, and Sharon rushed to distract her with a beaker of juice. That evening, she read the children a story then kissed them goodnight, leaving them giggling together at the novelty of sharing a room. Ten minutes later, silence reigned in the spare bedroom, and Sharon grinned at Gary.

'There you are — nothing to it. This won't be a problem.'

Gary handed her a glass of wine and they clinked. 'I didn't say it would be,' he said mildly. 'It's just not our chosen way of life, is it? Kids, playgroups, messy meal tables. But like you said, it's only a few weeks, and it'll be fun.'

And it was fun, thought Sharon, five weeks later as she stopped at the lights on the way home from the supermarket. She wasn't getting much work done, true, but she was thoroughly enjoying taking care of Ben and Katie. Being a mum to them, in fact. It almost made her wish...

But that wasn't going to happen. Only yesterday Gary was folding up Katie's buggy, and wondering what kind of contraption their own child would have 'in five or six years or so'. A twinge of regret made Sharon press her lips together. She rubbed her face, trying to ignore the tightness in her head. Five years was a long time... But they'd agreed to wait, so the best thing she could do was make sure Ben and Katie didn't worry or disturb Gary — that way, he'd realise that a child needn't mean the end of life as he knew it.

And so far, everything had worked out well. Ben and Katie were happy and healthy, and the 'elephant emails' were the highlights of each day. Gary was home in time for a story or a game before bed each evening, and when he and Sharon were going out, young Kelly next door was only too happy to babysit.

'Will there be another email when we get home?' Ben bounced up and down in his car seat.

'Might be. We'll check.' Sharon swung the car into their street and pulled up in the driveway, feeling her head swim as she got out and extracted Katie from her car seat.

'Right, Ben, love. I've got a bit of a headache – can you manage one of the bags for me? I'll take the other two, and Katie's big enough to walk all by herself, aren't you, darling?'

Ben obligingly lifted the smallest carrier from the boot and started up the steps to the front door. Katie, however, decided she wanted to be carried, and by the time Sharon had lugged two heavy bags and her niece to the kitchen, she felt as if she'd run a marathon backwards.

'Coffee,' she told herself firmly, sliding a cup under the machine. And a headache pill would help, too.

The children settled in front of the TV for their usual half hour of cartoons, and Sharon relaxed into the soft vastness of the sofa. A quick rest, and she'd be right as rain. If only she wasn't so hot...

'Sharon? You awake?'

Sharon blinked groggily into Gary's anxious face, and a stab of pain zipped through her head. She struggled upright and looked at the clock. *No* – she'd been asleep for over an hour.

'I – I don't... Ben!'

A chair scraped on the kitchen floor, and Ben appeared in the doorway. 'Here I am, Auntie Sharon. Katie was hungry so I made us banana sandwiches. Are you better now?'

'Better?' Gary reached out and touched her forehead. 'Good grief, you're burning up. Off to bed with you, and I'll bring you something to drink.'

Sharon started to argue, then realised she didn't have the energy. She crawled into bed and lay listening to Gary and the children, feeling as if she was floating on some kind of aircraft, the engines buzzing and burring in her head. Presently, she fell asleep.

When she awoke, Gary was tiptoeing about the room, and her throat felt on fire.

'It's okay, everything's under control,' he said. 'Kelly came over and helped put the kids to bed. Her mum says there's a two-day bug doing the rounds; that's probably what you've got. I've arranged to take a couple of days off work to look after the children – and I'll be able to get the new computer up and going, and paint the garden furniture, and reorganise the tool shed too.'

Sharon lay in bed, sucking a throat lozenge and feeling water from the too-damp cloth Gary had brought for her head trickle behind her ears. This was exactly what should never have happened. Kelly had college all day, so Gary would be looking after Katie and Ben by himself. The new computer was a desktop; if Gary got it out the box he'd be doing well, and the thought of the chaos Katie could create in the tool shed was almost enough to make Sharon laugh. As for painting – no sensible parent did that with their four and almost-two-year-olds within ten miles.

Gary was going to realise what having kids meant, and it might be enough to put him off for life. And Sharon knew now she simply couldn't wait to have a family of her own. Her baby – hers and Gary's. And then another, soon afterwards. And maybe even a third...

She sank back into a troubled sleep, and dreamt that Katie was emptying the fridge, and Ben was dressed as a question mark, tripping her up all the time.

The next morning Sharon swung her legs to the floor, determined to get up and help Gary with the children. But after five minutes on her feet she was only too glad to lie flat in bed again.

'I'm going to help Uncle Gary with the shopping and then we're going to get the new computer ready,' Ben announced from the doorway. 'Uncle Gary says the new computer's got much more space for photos and stuff. Why has it, Auntie Sharon? It doesn't look any bigger than usual.'

'I think it's sort of bigger inside,' said Sharon weakly.

Ben nodded. 'Like the Tardis,' he said, glancing over his shoulder. 'Hey, Uncle Gary! Don't dress Katie yet, she always has breakfast in her pyjamas because she's so messy.'

Ben vanished, and Sharon lay listening to the sounds coming from the kitchen. Gary had raspberry jam on his shirt when he put his head round the door to say they were off to the supermarket.

'Want anything?' He sounded calm enough.

'More throat pastilles. And some yoghurt,' Sharon croaked. 'And don't forget Ben has playgroup at half past one. You can put Katie down for her sleep before you drop him off; I can listen for her.'

She half-dozed all morning, only vaguely aware of Gary and the children returning. At lunchtime Gary brought her a yoghurt, looking rather pleased with himself.

Sharon blinked. Was he really carrying out his programme? 'How's the new computer coming on?'

'Haven't started yet. Ben wanted to make a boat with the box, so I had to find one for Katie, too. They've been playing with these. Maybe later, while Ben's at playgroup.'

Unfortunately, this turned out to be one of the days when Katie didn't have a lunchtime nap. She lay in her cot while Gary took Ben to playgroup, but as soon as he was back she shouted to get up again.

'I'll take her out to the garden,' said Gary, putting Sharon's mobile on the bedside table. 'Text if you need anything.'

The bedroom was at the back of the house, and Sharon lay listening as Gary – ably assisted by Katie – removed the garden furniture from the shed and set it on the patio. Surely he wasn't going to attempt a painting session... After a few minutes the voices faded away, and Sharon slept.

It was almost five when she woke to find Gary setting fresh water by her bed.

'Ah, no – we got everything out, but then Katie found that old aquarium, so we made a snail garden in it,' he said, in answer to her question. 'She's showing Ben now. I'm–'

A shriek from the garden made them both jump.

'Uncle Gary! Katie's knocked the bucket of coal over!'

Gary shot off, and Sharon sighed ruefully. She'd said at the time that a bucket wasn't the best place for the remains of the charcoal from last week's barbie.

The next day she was feeling slightly better, and managed to walk through and collapse on an armchair for a few hours. The coffee table had been shoved to one side to make space for the box boats, and Ben's Lego was strewn all over the floor. The kitchen was a sticky mess, and Gary put Katie's jeans into a hot wash and turned everything pale blue. And the normally cooperative Ben had a fit of the sulks because Gary made rice instead of pasta for lunch.

Sharon watched patient expression after patient expression cross Gary's face, and despaired. He would probably want to give up the whole idea of a baby, now.

By the time evening came she was feeling much better, and sat flipping through a magazine while

Gary bathed the children and organised them onto the sofa for the bedtime story.

'We didn't get an elephant email today,' said Ben suddenly, looking over to the desk, where the new computer was still waiting.

'Don't worry,' said Gary. 'I expect there'll be one tomorrow. We can look at all the photos again on the new monitor; we'll see them much better than on the laptop.' His shoulders were slumped with fatigue, and his hair looked positively wild.

Sharon felt a rush of pity for him. 'I'm sure I'll be well enough to look after Katie while you boys get the new computer ready,' she said, seeing the relieved expression that crossed Gary's face.

By nine o'clock Sharon was in bed, not knowing whether to laugh or cry. Gary had followed her through almost immediately, and was now snoring gently beside her.

'Uncle Gary! Uncle Gary!'

Sharon opened her eyes cautiously and peered across to Gary's side of the bed. Ben was there, determinedly shaking his uncle's shoulder.

'Wha – what is it, Ben?'

'Uncle Gary, let's do the computer now, before Katie wakes up. The big hand's nearly at the top, look!'

Ben thrust his Micky Mouse clock under Gary's nose, and a wild desire to laugh almost choked Sharon.

Gary had never sounded so patient. 'You're right. Thing is, Ben, we really should wait until the little hand's about here, see? Then it'll be seven o'clock. It's only three now. You scoot back to bed and wake me again when the little hand's at seven, there's a good chap.'

'Okay!' Ben disappeared again.

Next morning, Sharon was almost back to her usual self, and organised a 'who can gather the most Lego' game with Katie while Gary and Ben started on the computer. She was in the kitchen sorting out the chaos in the cutlery drawer when a triumphant whoop came from the living room.

'Auntie Sharon! *Two* elephant emails!'

Sharon rushed through. The first email had come yesterday evening, to say that the project was now running successfully, and Jill and Bruce would be home in a few days. The second, sent just half-an-hour ago, said they would be landing at Heathrow on Saturday evening. The day after tomorrow.

Sharon blinked back hot, sudden tears, looking at the stars in Ben and Katie's eyes. Mummy was coming home...

Time flew past after that. There was the children's packing to do, and Jill and Bruce's home, a 1930s semi on the other side of town, to air. Sharon and Katie did a supermarket shop for Jill and Bruce, and Gary printed out all the elephant emails and photos, which he and Ben organised into a folder.

Six o'clock on Saturday saw them waiting at the airport.

'Mummy! Daddy!' Ben ran, followed by Katie, and a huge lump rose in Sharon's throat. Lucky, lucky Jill, lucky Bruce. How wonderful to have two amazing kids over the moon to see you again.

And how empty home seemed that evening. Sharon started to clear the spare room, then realised she was exhausted, and flopped down on the sofa with a book. Gary came through with two glasses of wine.

'I'll get started on the garden furniture tomorrow,' he said. 'Two coats should do. We can invite some people over next weekend, now the kids have gone home.'

Sharon nodded listlessly. How glad he must be to have his life back again. No twenty questions about every move he made, no tiny fingers into everything he put down.

'Good idea. We can get back to normal, now,' she said.

He stared at her with a comical expression. 'Yes. And you know what – I don't want to! These past few weeks have been great. I honestly didn't know how much fun you could have with kids around. Sharon, I know we said we'd wait a few more years, but don't you think...?'

Sharon jerked upright. 'Oh, yes!'

They clinked glasses, and Sharon knew the stars were in her eyes now.

Patiently Waiting...

Gwen was beautiful. And kind. And gentle. And funny, too.

I noticed all this in about three seconds when I opened my eyes after the operation. After that, it only took another two to fall hopelessly in love with her.

I felt really silly about that operation – having one's tonsils removed at the grand old age of twenty-four isn't exactly glamorous, or heroic. In fact, most people seemed to find it downright funny.

Even my mother only just managed to conceal a smile before commiserating with me, and Lee, my youngest cousin, promptly lent me her teddy bear (newly re-christened 'Tonsil') to take into hospital with me. It was all pretty embarrassing.

'Never mind, Mike,' said Ron, my best mate, when he'd finished laughing. 'You won't have tonsillitis ever again. And maybe you'll meet a nice nurse.'

Then I opened my eyes after the operation – and saw Gwen, with her gorgeous curly dark hair, and that smile.

'Don't try to talk yet,' she said, wiping my face with a damp cloth. 'You can have something to drink soon. Just relax.'

I nodded and blinked at her, and I tried to smile, but it felt as though my throat was full of needles. I read her name badge. Staff Nurse Gwen Rodgers. My heart was beating so fast I was surprised she didn't notice.

She propped Lee's teddy up against my pillow and smiled at me, a real, warm smile. 'Does he have a name?'

'Tonsil,' I croaked, and she giggled.

'Very apt.'

Her brown eyes laughed into mine, and suddenly our hands touched. A shiver ran right through me. Had she felt it, too? I watched as she went round the other five patients in the room, and by the time she was finished, I knew that my mission in life was to marry Gwen and live happily ever after. Funny. I'd never believed in love at first sight – but now I knew different...

Gwen paused at the door, and our eyes met. A huge surge of hope welled up inside me. She felt the same; I was sure she did.

My tonsils were apparently more complicated than most, so I had to stay in overnight – but now I didn't mind. It would give me the chance to see more of Gwen... Should I ask her out now, or wait until I was discharged?

I slept for the next couple of hours, and when I woke again a different set of nurses was on duty. One of them brought me a bowl of ice cream and chivvied me into the chair, and another appeared to help make my bed. Student Nurse Anne Page and Student Nurse Laura Winter, I saw from their badges, and started on my ice cream.

They chatted for a moment about Sister's new shoes, and then...

'Have you seen Gwen's ring yet?' Annie flapped the bottom sheet across to Laura, who pulled it straight. They both made efficient hospital corners at the top of the mattress.

I froze, a spoonful of ice cream halfway to my mouth.

'It's gorgeous, isn't it?' Laura plumped up my pillows. 'Isn't it sweet how she wears it on a chain round her neck?'

'I've never seen such beautiful emeralds,' said Annie, dreamily. 'And that diamond!'

Automatically, I put my spoonful of ice cream into my mouth. Strawberry ice cream, when my whole world was crumbling in front of me. Was Gwen engaged?

'She told me all about it,' said Laura. 'That Reginald – do you know he went down on one knee, proposing?'

'A real proper proposal!' giggled Annie. 'Not many do that nowadays!'

They finished the bed and turned to me.

'Why, Mike,' said Laura. 'You've gone quite pale. Back into bed. I'll just get Sister.'

Sister came and took my pulse, peered at my

throat, and gave me some ice to suck – none of which made the slightest difference to the desolation in my heart. Within five hours, I'd fallen in love, planned the rest of my life – and then had it yanked away from me. Had I imagined the look Gwen had given me? That feeling of togetherness?

She was just being a good nurse, I told myself fiercely. And you're a stupid fool.

The next morning I was given the all clear to go home. Gwen, on duty again, brought me a little paper bag with my medicines.

'Lozenges for your throat, no more than twelve a day,' she instructed, her eyes gazing warmly into mine. 'And some painkillers. Drink plenty, and no curries for a while!'

She grinned, and I forced myself to smile. Oh, Gwen. We could have been good together. But Gwen loved someone called Reginald who'd gone down on one knee to propose. We walked to the lift side by side, and I pressed the button. Our eyes met... but what could I say, except goodbye, and thank you?

'It was a pleasure,' she said, I noticed that her eyes were suddenly brighter. She blew her nose, and the lift came, and I stepped in.

'Bye,' I said, through clenched teeth.

She raised her hand in a wave, the doors closed, and down I went. It was the worst moment of my life.

Mum was waiting in the car park – I was going to stay with her and Dad for the rest of the week to recuperate. She drove back, then followed me upstairs with a huge glass of iced tea.

'Drink,' she said firmly.

I drank; you didn't argue with Mum. She unpacked my bag while I sat on my old bed and watched. It was just like being a kid again.

'There's no sign of Lee's bear,' she said, checking through the things she'd taken from the bag. 'You haven't forgotten him, have you?'

I groaned, then stopped because it hurt my throat. I'd left poor Tonsil sitting in solitary splendour on the chair beside my bed in Ward 4c.

'She won't need him today,' said Mum consolingly. 'But they're all coming over on Saturday, so you'd better fetch him home before then.'

I didn't sleep well that night. Fetching Tonsil home would involve the additional torture of returning to the ward and maybe seeing Gwen again. And going through another painful goodbye scene. All I could be glad about was I hadn't made a fool of myself by asking her out. She didn't know how I felt about her – or did she? My cheeks burned at the thought.

In the end, I went back for Tonsil on Friday morning.

Nurse Laura was just inside the ward. 'Oh, what a pity!' she said, laughing. 'We're all very fond of him now.' She pointed to where Tonsil was sitting, on top of a filing cabinet in Sister's office. 'I'll just get someone. He's official Lost Property; you have to sign for him.'

She hurried off, and a moment later Gwen appeared from a side room.

'Hello, Mike.'

I swallowed. Her face – if I hadn't known about Reginald, I'd have said her face lit up when she saw me.

She took me into Sister's room, and slid a book towards me. I bent and signed blindly where she was pointing. Being so near her was doing things to my heart, and the smell of her perfume – faint, and flowery – made me feel almost giddy. I straightened up quickly, and caught a glimpse of a delicate gold chain round her neck. The chain for Reginald's ring...

Again, there was nothing to say except goodbye and thank you.

'You're welcome,' she said, her voice trembling.

I tucked Tonsil under my arm and turned to the ward doors.

'Mike!' she called suddenly, and I turned. 'It's the hospital Garden Fair tomorrow,' she said, almost wildly. 'We – the ward – are doing the cake stall. Maybe your family...'

'Sounds great – I'll tell them. See you there, then!' I gabbled, and almost ran from the ward. Brilliant. Now I'd have to see her again, and say goodbye for a third time.

I glared at Tonsil. 'This is all your fault.'

Lee and her family arrived before lunch the following day. I told Lee that Tonsil had stayed two days extra in hospital because he'd enjoyed the ice cream so much.

'Oh,' she said, hugging him fiercely. 'Well, he's better now and his name's Pooh again 'cos he likes honey best.' She stomped off towards the garden.

'I don't think she'd lend him out again,' Doris, Lee's mum, said, laughing. 'She was a sorry child that first night. Only the thought of poor Mike in hospital, really *needing* a bear, could console her.'

We all laughed, but a warm feeling inside me eased the ache of losing Gwen, just a little. Lee was family, and she loved me enough to lend me something she treasured.

It was Mum's suggestion that we go to the hospital fair. I'd decided to forget about it, and try to forget Gwen, too – how impossible – but two o'clock saw us all walking into the hospital grounds. I hadn't been on a family outing like this for years. There was Mum and Dad, Doris and Jim, me, Lee, and Tonsil. Sorry, Pooh.

'Let's meet at the tea tent at half past three,' said Mum, pulling Doris towards the handwork display. 'Look after Lee, will you, Mike?'

Dad and Jim had disappeared, so I didn't have much choice. Lee and I wandered around. We had a go at the wheelchair obstacle course, played walking stick hockey, and guessed the weight of a bedpan filled with plaster bandages. And all the time I was trying to decide how to react if we saw Gwen.

In the end, I was so busy daydreaming about meeting her that I almost fell over her.

'Mike!' She grabbed my arm just in time to stop me colliding with her trolleyful of cakes. She wasn't in uniform today, and she looked incredible in a pale-yellow top over black jeans. My mouth went dry as we stared at each other.

'I'm Lee, who are you?'

No one could ever accuse my cousin of shyness.

Gwen looked down at her and laughed. 'I'm Gwen. I see you've brought Tonsil along too.'

'His name's Pooh again now. You can hold him if you like.'

Gwen took Tonsil/Pooh, and all at once I noticed the large, old-fashioned diamond and emerald ring on the third finger of her right hand. Her *right* hand. I stood there stupidly. What could it mean? Wasn't she...? And Reginald...? I didn't know what to think.

Meanwhile, Gwen and Lee were having a conversation about teddies.

'You're right, Pooh's a better name for a bear. Mike was very glad to have him in hospital, you know!' Gwen laughed up at me.

I couldn't stand it any longer. I thrust some coins at Lee and told her to go and buy some ice cream. Then I grabbed Gwen's right hand. 'Gwen—' I stopped, because the words were choking me.

'Mike, what is it?' She was gripping my hand so hard it was almost painful.

I touched her ring with one finger. 'Gwen, who is Reginald?'

And in a second her whole face was bright with hope. 'He was my grandfather,' she said slowly. 'He and Granny met seventy years ago, and they were engaged within a week. She died last month and I miss her terribly. Having her ring means so much.'

I've never felt like I did at that moment. Love, hope, joy, happiness – it was the dizziest feeling I've ever had.

'I thought–' Again, I stopped, because the only thing that mattered right then was kissing her, so I did.

And straightaway I knew that everything was going to be all right. I knew that in seventy years' time I would still love Gwen, and she would still love me.

All the same, I couldn't let Reginald get the better of me, could I? He was obviously a bloke who knew how to do things properly. I dropped to one knee, still holding Gwen's hand.

'Gwen, I love you. Will you marry me?'

She laughed, and bent to kiss me again. 'I thought you'd never ask,' she whispered.

Nothing Stays the Same

The train jerked, then creaked forwards. Diane's eyes filled with hot tears, and she blinked impatiently. 'Bye, darling,' she called, not knowing if Nadia, inside the train, would hear her. 'Have fun – and take care! Phone us tomorrow night! Be–'

Nadia waved, a huge grin on her face as the train picked up speed. Diane waved back frantically, aware of Colin beside her doing exactly the same. She stepped back – she could still see Nadia's face – but then... her girl was gone.

Colin patted her shoulder. 'Come on, love. Let's have coffee in that new place with the squishy cakes. Plenty of time before we need to go home.' His voice was gruff, and he cleared his throat loudly.

Diane fell into step beside him. Yes, they had plenty of time, because there was no one left at home now. No one needing her. She had just seen her youngest child off on what was surely life's biggest adventure, the first job away from home. Nadia was off to London on her own, to share a flat with two other girls Diane had only met once.

She glanced up at Colin's solemn face. It was difficult for him, too. Nadia was their only daughter and the apple of her father's eye. They were both really going to miss her.

The house was silent when they arrived home. And it was filled with so many reminders of Nadia. Everywhere Diane looked there was something. The book Nadia had just finished. Her old jacket, hanging in the hallway. Even the smell of her perfume still lingered in the bathroom. In a way, these things were comforting, but they could never change the fact that her daughter was gone. Thank goodness it was Saturday, and neither of them had to go to work.

Diane did her Saturday chores, her heart heavy. She was tidying up after Nadia for the last time. No happy, exuberant, bubbly daughter would fish around in these drawers tonight, looking for something to wear, and for the first Saturday night since goodness knows when, Diane wouldn't have to lie awake, listening for Nadia's key in the door. She sighed, and swallowed hard.

It must be like this for everyone when their family left the nest, she thought glumly. You loved them and took care of them all those years, and then suddenly your job was over and they were gone. It was natural – a good thing, in a way. But it still felt very lonely. She didn't really feel like a mum any longer.

'Of course you're still a mum!' protested Colin at dinner time, when Diane confided her thoughts. 'You're Joe's mum and Nadia's mum, and that will never change. You're feeling down in the dumps and

I know exactly the thing for you.' He refused to say more, but when Diane was loading plates into the dishwasher, he poked his head round the kitchen door and announced he'd be back in half an hour. He was, too, but he wouldn't tell her what he'd been up to.

The following morning, Colin was up first and had breakfast ready when Diane came downstairs. He grinned at her.

'Lazybones. Here's your coffee. Now, we'll have no time to mope around today – look!'

He pointed to a large box by the back door. Diane went to investigate, and saw several tubs of paint as well as a selection of brushes and rollers.

'Yellow paint, for the kitchen!' she cried, remembering how she'd moaned just last week that magnolia was a boring colour and that the kitchen ought to be a lot brighter.

'Right,' said Colin. 'Now get that toast inside you, and we'll start work straightaway.'

He held her close for a moment, and Diane hugged back, comforted. It was a good idea. It was so hard not to think of Nadia all the time. Where was she now? Asleep in bed, probably. Well, she had promised to call them tonight.

It was surprising how quickly they managed to transform the kitchen. Colin rollered the walls and ceiling while Diane did the paintwork, and the washing machine sloshed the curtains round. They stopped for a sandwich at one o'clock, and by four the kitchen was the sunniest yellow Diane had ever seen. She looked round approvingly.

'It's like one of those home improvement programmes on telly! Well, almost. And I'm starving!'

Colin banged the lid shut on the tub of paint. They'd barely used half. 'Let's treat ourselves to some pub grub,' he suggested. 'We'll be back in plenty of time for Nadia's call at nine.'

Nadia! Diane realised guiltily that she'd barely given her daughter a thought all day. The ache was still there in the background, of course, but everyday life – painting the kitchen – had prevented them from moping. How clever Colin was.

By the time they reached the coffee stage after their meal, Diane was feeling well-fed and almost content. Nadia would phone in an hour or so, and tell them all about the flat and her flatmates. And tomorrow Diane would make up a parcel with a few little luxuries from home. Nadia would like that.

'I'll just get myself a brandy, as a treat,' said Colin. 'Want one?'

Diane shook her head. She sipped her coffee and caught a snatch of conversation as two women went by.

'–and she looks so different with that hair colour – I hardly recognised her.'

Diane smiled to herself. It was amazing what a bit of colour could do, for people as well as rooms. Her kitchen was almost unrecognisable, too.

All at once, she felt cold all over. Unrecognisable.

They had turned their old, familiar, family kitchen into something new and different. Something Nadia would hardly recognise. Somehow, that didn't feel so good any more.

Diane was silent all the way home, and so was Colin. Was he having doubts too?

The paint was dry when they arrived back, and the kitchen did look lovely. But it was no longer the kitchen Nadia would be picturing when she phoned them.

Colin was looking round approvingly. 'Good job, well done,' he said. 'Now, I've been thinking. Joe's settled in Edinburgh, he doesn't need a room for himself here. And Nadia will only be home for weekends and holidays now. Why don't we make Joe's room into a kind of guest room for them both, and turn Nadia's room into a workroom? You could leave the sewing machine up – and we could shift the computer out of the dining room.'

Diane stared at him. She'd wanted a computer-free dining room for ages. And it would be lovely not to have to start from scratch every time she used the sewing machine. But...

'No!' she cried, banging her fist on the table. 'I won't have it! You can't clean and rearrange our children out of our home – out of our lives!'

'But–' Colin protested, sheer dismay on his face.

'No!' insisted Diane, and at that moment the phone rang.

Heart thumping, Diane settled down on the sofa to talk to her daughter. How near Nadia sounded, and how normal. She chatted on about her new room, and the film she'd seen last night, and how kind her flatmates were being.

'That's wonderful, darling. I'm so pleased,' said Diane. 'I'll make you up a little parcel tomorrow. I'm going to bake some ginger snaps.'

'Great,' said Nadia. 'And tell me – how do you like your new kitchen?'

Diane blinked. 'You know about it?'

Nadia giggled. 'Dad and I planned it in advance. I told him what colour you'd like, and what would match the curtains. Is it nice?'

'Um – it's lovely,' said Diane, completely taken aback. 'I was just worrying about you hardly recognizing the place, actually.'

Nadia laughed again. 'Don't worry, Mum. Home's still home and always will be, even when I've got a home of my own and six kids. It's the people that count – you and Dad! Has he told you about the plan for my old bedroom?'

'Yes,' Diane admitted. 'I wasn't too happy about it, but maybe...'

'Go for it,' said Nadia. 'You don't need more than one spare bedroom. Spread yourselves around and enjoy the place!'

After handing the phone over to Colin, Diane wandered back into the kitchen. Nadia and Colin were right. And the love and the memories would always be here, no matter what they did with the rooms. It was time for a change.

Colin came in and looked at her questioningly. 'We

don't need to do anything you're not happy about.'

Diane leaned back against the sink. 'We'll do it,' she said thoughtfully. 'We can go over Joe's room with the leftover paint from the kitchen. It'll be a nice cheerful room for him or Nadia when they visit. And when they're both here—'

'The computer and the sewing machine can go back into the dining room!' Colin hugged her.

Diane picked up the half-empty tub of paint. 'Come on, then,' she said mischievously. 'What are we waiting for?'

We're Having a Baby!

I felt as if I was walking on air that day – the day of the pregnancy test. It was a Friday, and Susie came down for breakfast looking a bit shell-shocked.

'It's positive,' she said, her voice trembling.

It took me a moment to realise what she was saying. 'Positive? You mean–'

She flung herself into my arms. 'We're having a baby! Oh, Rory!'

To say I was proud as Punch would be the understatement of the century. Here I was, twenty-eight years old, newly-promoted to assistant head of the Supplies Department at Mercer's in town, married just six months to the girl of my dreams – with a baby on the way! Everything would be different now – I'd be a dad soon, and it was going to be great.

The trouble was, everyone except Susie thought it was the most enormous joke.

'A baby? You'd better buy a doll to practise on, Rory, or you'll be dropping the poor little thing all over the place!' Joe, my boss, was grinning from ear to ear.

'You? A baby? Poor Susie, she'll have her hands full with a baby to look after as well as watching out for you!' My brother Paul, who worked in the same company, had to sit down, he was laughing so hard.

Okay, so I was a bit accident-prone. Things just seemed to happen to me, somehow. But that would all change when I was a dad. Dads were automatically serious, responsible people, weren't they? So there was no need to make remarks like Joe and Paul had.

After work that day, I went to give Mum the good news. She wouldn't consider being a grandma again a joke. I could count on her not to laugh.

I was right – she didn't laugh. A positively apprehensive expression froze itself onto her face, and she sat down suddenly.

'A baby! Oh, Rory – you will be careful, won't you?'

The only person in the world who seemed to think I was capable of coping with a baby was Susie. We cuddled up on the sofa one evening, marvelling at the first ultra-sound picture of our son or daughter and making plans.

'We'll go to all the classes,' Susie said dreamily. 'And I'll get the grans knitting some cute little cardies – a September baby will need lots of cardies. And I'll buy a names book in town tomorrow.'

'I'll get the family cradle from my sister,' I said. 'And I'll paint the spare room, of course – the baby's room, I mean.'

Susie looked up at me. 'Dad could give you a hand. He'd enjoy it.'

I shook my head. This was my – our – baby. I

wanted to do things for it myself. Susie understood, but Ted, her father, wasn't so sure.

'Rory, the last time you had a paintbrush in your hand, the garden shed turned out sky blue instead of brown,' he pointed out. 'Apart from the bit where you ran out of paint, that is.'

I frowned. 'I misread the label, that's all. Susie liked it, so I left it. And it wasn't my fault the wood soaked up more paint than it should have, and the shop had discontinued the colour when I went for more. It could have happened to anyone.'

'Yes, but it happened to *you*,' he retorted meaningfully.

So I took great care about choosing paint for the baby's room. Plain white for the walls, and a nice sunshiny yellow for the woodwork. And we were getting a new carpet, too. The baby would love it.

I set to work one Saturday, and soon had the walls covered. Perfect! I stood back to admire my handiwork, then turned to look at the yellow paint, a tiny doubt worming its way into my head. Did I really have enough? One pot didn't seem much when you considered it had to cover the door, too. Maybe I should go for more.

Susie had taken the car round to her mother's, so I grabbed my bike from the garage and set off. At the first corner I remembered that I still hadn't fixed the right brake; it was one of those fiddly jobs that was all too easy to put off. Oh, well, never mind. The bike was still perfectly ridable, and I didn't have far to go.

I spent an enjoyable half hour wandering around

the DIY store, buying a couple of shelves for the baby's room and a new hammer as well as the tub of paint. Getting me and my purchases onto the bike was a bit of a challenge, mind you. If I'd known I was going to be buying so much stuff, I'd have waited for Susie and the car. But eventually, everything was securely tied on, and I set off.

The journey went swimmingly until I was zooming down the little hill just before our street. I tried to brake for the turn, but of course, only one brake was working. So round the corner I went at almost full speed, executing a frightful wobble to avoid our neighbour's new car. I bounced across the pavement and fell right into the middle of Susie's hydrangea bush. The pot of yellow paint escaped its moorings, described a lovely arc through the air and landed on my left ear – and opened.

'Oh, well, Rory, at least you got it all off eventually,' Susie said comfortingly that evening, applying more cream to my poor afflicted ear. 'And there's still quite a lot of paint left in the pot. I'm sure we'll have enough.'

We did, but the episode did nothing for my confidence. Dads weren't supposed to have stupid accidents like that, were they? Old Mrs Henderson next door had seen the whole thing from her dining room window, and laughed so much she'd had to go for a lie down afterwards. I didn't want to be laughable...

In the weeks that followed, I tried very hard to be steady and sensible. Somehow, though, something always went wrong. I helped Susie pick out a pram, and the handle jammed while I was trying to fold the wretched thing up to get it into the boot. When we were choosing a changing table, I banged heads – hard – with the shop assistant while he was showing me how to convert it into a chest of drawers for later. Worst of all, the handle on the carrier bag broke in the middle of the shopping centre car park after our big 'baby-shop', and all the dummies and muslins and bottles and bibs and wipes rolled merrily all over the place, and there I was, scrabbling around after them while cars queued up behind me.

Oh, people were kind. Not your fault, Rory, they said. But an insistent little voice in my head was telling me I was going to be the most useless, butter-fingered dad on the planet. How was I going to cope with a real live baby, when I couldn't even manage inanimate objects like prams and carrier bags?

And there was still the new carpet to be laid. We'd ordered it ages ago, a lovely colourful blobby pattern, perfect for a child's room. Unfortunately, there was a problem with the suppliers, and it didn't arrive until two weeks before the baby was due. And when it did arrive, my carpet-layer friend Jim, who was supposed to be helping me, was away on holiday.

I looked at the carpet, rolled up at the side of the baby's room, and took a deep breath. This was my chance to show everyone that I really was a sensible, fatherly figure now. And laying carpets wasn't difficult – I'd done a couple with Jim and we'd never had any problems. I rolled up my sleeves.

And to my secret surprise, the new carpet positively floated down on the floor. I worked my way round the edge, finishing it off at the skirting board.

Susie looked in as I was passing the first corner. 'Wow, that was quick! It looks great.'

I tried not to look smug. 'Nothing to it. Come and talk to me while I'm doing the rest?'

She shook her head. 'I'm going for a bath. I'm hoping the hot water will ease this sore back I've had all day.'

She waddled off, and I worked my way up the side of the room. Two more weeks and the baby would be here, using the crib and the changing table... what an incredible thought. The carpet continued to be cooperative, and I was nearly back at the start when I heard Susie get out the bath. Good. I would finish this and then I'd put the kettle on.

I should have known my luck wouldn't last. There I was, literally at the last two centimetres, when my hand slipped and the knife sliced painfully into my left thumb.

'Ouch!' I grabbed a tissue and wound it round my thumb, and did the last bit one-handedly, trying not to drip blood on the new carpet. But it was finished, and it looked very–

'Rory!'

Susie's voice had me running to the bathroom, almost falling over the cot and changing table parked on the landing. I'd never heard her sound like that. She was sitting on the edge of the bath in her dressing gown, both hands clutching her bump, her face pale.

'Rory, the baby's coming!'

'What? When – do you–' I danced round clutching my thumb.

Fortunately, Susie kept her head. 'Get my case, and let's go. It's been just the two contractions so far, but they were only a few minutes apart.'

I grabbed a wad of kitchen paper for my thumb in passing, and drove as quickly as I dared to the hospital, Susie stifling her groans beside me and my thumb throbbing all the time. But we made it.

'Well, this one's in a hurry!' said the midwife, examining Susie. 'But it's all looking good, don't worry.' She patted my shoulder as she passed. 'What's up with your thumb, Rory?'

I opened my mouth to reply, but a loud moan from Susie distracted both me and the midwife from my wretched thumb. Things moved quickly after that, and I was kept busy holding Susie's hand and wiping her face – and then there was a huge flurry of activity and amazingly, incredibly, our baby girl was there, making funny little new-baby yowls and looking absolutely gorgeous. I'm not ashamed to say there were tears running down my cheeks.

I hugged Susie as hard as I dared. 'Oh love, look – it's our Miriam!'

Susie's eyes were shining like the sun. 'Isn't she beautiful? Rory, isn't she just perfect?'

And we sat there, the three of us, a family at last, and I was so glad they were both all right, my girls.

After a while the midwife came back and swooped down on me. 'Right, now we've a minute to look at that thumb.' She grabbed it and unwrapped my kitchen paper bandage. 'Heavens, Rory, this is quite deep. You'll need a couple of stitches.'

She bundled me off to A&E while the doctor came to check on Susie and Miriam. I was allowed to skip the queue a bit, and half an hour later I was on my way back to Maternity, a large white bandage on my stitched-up thumb and the A&E staff's congratulations ringing in my ears.

Susie was in a different room now, and all our parents were gathered around, doting-grandparent expressions on their faces. Miriam was fast asleep in one of those fish tank baby cots.

'Well, lad, what have you been up to?' Ted slapped my back.

'Congratulations, darling,' said Mum, kissing me. 'But for goodness' sake, be more careful with my granddaughter than you are with your thumbs!'

The grandparents all laughed, and suddenly I felt extremely foolish. I'd done it again, hadn't I? My daughter was here now, and I still wasn't sensible and responsible. As if she could feel my misery, Miriam awoke and began to howl lustily.

Ted lifted her. 'Now then, lass. Easy does it.' He cradled her expertly in his arms, but the howls went on.

'Give her to me,' Dad said. 'Maybe she doesn't like your aftershave.'

He took her, but the howls continued, and Susie looked at me appealingly.

'Um – I'll take her,' I said, but Mum stepped

forward and relieved Dad of his bundle.

'There, there, darling.' She jiggled Miriam in the way that only proper mums can. Miriam howled on.

'I've always been good with babies,' Susie's mum said, getting in on the act and rocking Miriam to her chest while Susie's eyes pleaded with me from the bed.

'Give her to Rory, Mum,' she said, her voice trembling.

I stepped forward as confidently as I could. Susie had done all the hard work, and if she wanted me to hold our baby, then I would, though my heart was pounding away as if I'd just run a marathon backwards.

My daughter was howling indignantly, her eyes screwed shut. I gathered her into both arms, awkwardly because of my thumb, aware that all four grandparents were hovering anxiously. I looked down at Miriam.

And then fuzzy blue eyes were gazing into mine. The howls ceased abruptly, and the whole world seemed to stop while I stood there holding my baby girl as we looked at each other.

Ted broke the silence. 'Well, seems like she knows who her daddy is.'

'Yes. We'll leave you three to it, and visit again tomorrow,' said Mum. 'You're obviously coping.'

The four of them trooped out, and we were alone. I sat down beside Susie's bed, Miriam in my arms, and smiled at my wife. This was the best, the very best time of all. We had our whole lives in front of us

to share with this beautiful little girl, our Miriam.
And she knew who her daddy was...

Miles From Home

Martina Cameron pushed her jacket into the overhead locker and slid across to the window seat. Her bag was tucked securely under the seat in front, and she had a magazine, some tissues and a packet of chewing gum on her lap – she was ready. She fastened her seatbelt and sat back, idly watching her fellow passengers settle down.

The last time, the last time… A hurtful little voice in her head. Martina swallowed hard.

Hurtful or not, it was true. This would be the last time she would fly from Geneva to Edinburgh and find a home waiting for her. Her mother was moving to Bedford to live with Martina's brother Iain and his family. But home was in Edinburgh… wasn't it?

'Chewing gum?'

A voice broke into her daydream, and she looked up to see a young man sitting in the aisle seat.

'Oh – thank you. But I've got some too.' Martina lifted her magazine and produced her own packet.

'The same brand. Shall we be sociable and share mine taking off and yours landing, or shall we be independent and each chew our own?' He grinned, and Martina had to laugh.

'Oh, let's be sociable.' She accepted a piece of gum.

'Good. Don't worry, I won't talk you to death the whole flight,' he said, laying his pullover on the empty seat between them. 'Ah, we're off.'

Martina peered through her window and watched the airport building disappear behind them as they taxied to the runway. She sat back with a sigh as the plane gathered speed, and glanced across to see her companion pull a face as they lurched into the air.

His name was Jack, he told her, and he was PA to a businessman with offices in London and Geneva. Like her, he was Scottish, on his way now to spend a week with his sister in Edinburgh.

'I'll take the kids to the zoo, and so on,' he said happily. 'What about you?'

'I'm a nurse; I've been working in Geneva for three years now. It was only supposed to be one year, but the job's great, and it's lovely being able to travel around Europe when I'm off duty.'

Lovely, but selfish, she thought, and there it was again, the huge lump in her throat. If she'd stayed at home, Mum might not have had to leave Edinburgh for far-away Bedford, where she knew no one except Iain and his family. Guilt thudded into Martina's middle.

The plane veered sideways, and several people gasped. Martina chewed her gum hard.

'Okay?' said Jack.

She nodded, and he went back to his newspaper.

Eyes closed, Martina sat thinking about Edinburgh. Not as central as Geneva, maybe, but definitely not a bad place to live. Why hadn't she returned to Scotland long ago? She should have gone home as soon as her mother's arthritis worsened to the extent that she found living in a two-story house problematic. It wasn't as if nursing jobs in Edinburgh were in short supply. But – she'd wanted to stay in Geneva. Martina bit her lip.

You don't know what's important, do you? sneered her conscience. You've seen the Matterhorn and Mont Blanc, and you've been to Zurich and St Moritz and Salzburg and Rome, but you've lost your sense of family along the way.

A flight attendant offering lunch broke into the gloomy thoughts. Martina looked unenthusiastically at the tuna on wholemeal sandwich.

Jack was chewing already. 'How about some wine to go with this?'

Martina smiled back. He was such a happy, pleasant soul – it was impossible to snub him.

'White wine,' she said, and he passed over the little bottle from the attendant.

Martina started on her sandwich. 'How many children does your sister have?'

'Three. Aged nine, seven and four. Girl, boy, girl. She's divorced, so it's not easy for her. She has a flat in Corstorphine, and a job as a school secretary.'

Martina abandoned the sandwich and sat sipping her wine. 'Mum lives in Corstorphine too. At least, she did. She's moving to Bedford next week, to my brother's. That's why I'm going now.'

'A working holiday,' said Jack.

Martina nodded. They would be packing up Mum's treasures, all those little things holding memories of a happy family life. But there wouldn't be space for them all in Iain's granny flat. She closed her eyes again as the guilty thoughts swirled back.

By the time lunch was cleared away they were almost at Edinburgh, and Martina offered Jack some of her gum. The landing was uneventful, and Jack pushed his newspaper into the briefcase he pulled from the overhead locker.

'Nice meeting you,' he said, winking at her. 'Who knows, maybe we'll meet again someday, on the streets of Corstorphine, or Geneva. Good luck with the removal!'

He squeezed into the aisle and disappeared among the stream of passengers. Martina sighed. She hadn't been very chatty, had she, and he seemed so nice...

Her case was already circling on the luggage belt when she arrived at baggage reclaim, and Jack was nowhere to be seen. Martina hurried through customs and out into the busy hallway.

'Hi, there! You look great!' Iain hugged her hard, then let go for six-year-old Evan to take his place.

Martina looked out curiously during the short drive from the airport, but, as usual, nothing much had changed. Home was still home – for a day or two. The lump in her throat grew larger when Iain pulled up outside the semi the two of them had grown up in. This was where she had played her child's games, grown into a noisy teenager and then an ambitious young woman. Here, she'd gone through chickenpox and spots and the agonies of first love, and made her career choices. This was home… The front door opened, and Sophie Cameron appeared on the doorstep, a huge beam on her comfortable face.

'Mum!' There were more hugs and kisses before Martina was pulled into the living room and plied with questions about life in Geneva. She answered as well as she could, blinking at her mother as she saw how the older woman was drinking it all in. You'd never think Mum was about to go through her biggest upheaval in over thirty years.

'So – what happens now?' Martina looked round the room as Iain went to make coffee. Obviously, the packing hadn't been started yet.

'Work starts tomorrow,' said Sophie, laughing. 'Getting all this lot sorted and packed – I'm glad there are four of us to do it.'

Martina took her mother's hand. Maybe it wasn't too late. 'Mum – wouldn't you prefer to–'

But Iain came back with the coffee pot and an enormous chocolate cake. Evan shrieked with joy, and Martina's question remained unasked.

The next morning, they set to work. Martina armed herself with a duster, and packed her mother's four hundred or so books into crates.

'I have sorted them out!' said Sophie indignantly,

when Martina asked if she really wanted to take them all. 'I put four aside for the charity shop. A book is like an old friend, you know. I need them all.'

'She's having wall-to-wall bookcases in her new sitting room,' said Iain mischievously.

Martina felt as if her face was frozen. Her mother was taking these 'old friends' – but she was having to leave her real friends behind. And all because Martina had been too selfish to come home and take care of her. You're not a proper daughter, her conscience informed her. It's a wonder she's being so nice to you.

When the books were packed, Martina started on the ornaments, wrapping them in tissue paper and bedding them down in a large box. And oh, there were so many memories attached to these. The china dog from Aunt Liz, the rose bowl that had been a wedding present – they all had a story and Martina knew them all. They were part of her Edinburgh childhood.

By lunchtime, she had wallowed in nostalgia so thoroughly she could hardly speak.

Sophie noticed her pale face. 'You need a breath of fresh air,' she said. 'Why don't you take Evan into town for a hamburger? You could walk through the gardens and look at the castle, too, and do the shopping on the way home.'

Martina agreed. If she went out for a while, she might get things into perspective. Her mother obviously wasn't unhappy about going to Bedford – but wouldn't she have *preferred* to stay in her own home?

Princes Street was busy as usual. Evan wanted to

go for lunch first, so they found a hamburger place that met with his approval. Martina battled through the crowd to order, and brought their tray back to Evan at a sticky table.

'Makes airline food seem positively civilised, doesn't it?' The voice from behind came as she was biting into her cheeseburger. Martina turned quickly, losing a chunk of cucumber in the process, and saw Jack, sitting at the next table with three ketchup-covered children. Martina had to laugh when she looked at them, and Jack produced a packet of wipes and shook his head at her.

'You may laugh, young lady, but I've done this before, you know. A couple of wipes and they'll be good as new,' he said, cleaning the youngest child's chin while the others wiped themselves. 'Let me introduce my family – Carol, Al, and little Zoe.'

'My sister's called Zoe, too,' said Evan immediately. 'She's just two and she's at home with my mum in Bedford.'

Soon all four children were talking at once, and Jack packed away his wipes and looked hopefully at Martina. 'Fancy a stroll in the gardens? We've got a Frisbee.'

Even gulped the remainder of his milk shake and leapt to his feet. 'Come on, Martina!'

They crossed over to the gardens, and Martina and Jack found a bench and sat down while Carol took charge of the Frisbee. Jack leaned forwards, arms on his thighs.

'Tell me it's none of my business, but you don't

look like you're having a great time. Do you want to talk about it?'

Martina fought to hold the tears back. 'I –' She fumbled for a tissue.

Jack handed her one from his packet. 'Telling an almost-stranger might help, you know.'

Martina dabbed her eyes. 'I just feel so guilty – Mum's moving to Bedford and it's all my fault.' The whole story came out – how she loved living in Geneva, and how impossible it seemed to talk to her mother about it.

Jack listened, saying nothing until she stopped. 'Don't you think your mother would have asked – or at least said something about it – if she'd wanted to stay in Edinburgh?'

'I don't know.' Martina sat picking at her tissue. 'I've been too scared to mention it in case she asked me to come home. That's how horrible I am.'

'You're not horrible. But you have to talk to your mother. You'll be miserable until you do.'

He was right; Martina knew it. She couldn't keep avoiding the issue. She would talk to her mother that very afternoon. Happier now the decision was made, she gave Jack a shaky smile.

'Thanks. You've been very understanding and helpful.'

Jack raised his eyebrows. 'Well, that's a first.'
'What is?'

He stared up at the castle. 'Someone calling me understanding. I find it hard to talk to people, so I joke to cover my nerves. Everyone thinks I'm just a clown.'

Martina touched his arm quickly. Her turn to hand out a few words of encouragement. 'I think you just need practise.'

He shrugged, then grinned. 'Maybe I do. How about helping me practise again tomorrow? The kids are bosom buddies now, seems a pity to limit that to one game of Frisbee.'

Home again, Martina put the shopping into the fridge and went to find her mother.

Sophie was upstairs in the spare bedroom, sorting through bed linen. 'I won't take much of this; the rest can go to the charity shop. Or shall we put some in a box for you? You might want it some day.'

Martina sank down on the bed and took a deep breath. Now for it. 'Mum – I know I'm a bit late saying this – but if I left Geneva we could stay on here, together.'

Her mother glared. 'Heavens – what kind of mother do you think I am? I don't want you to leave your own life to help me with mine. You just keep sending me those wonderful photos from exotic places, and be happy. That's all I want.'

'Really?' Tears sprang into Martina's eyes.

Sophie sat down too, and hugged her. 'Yes, really. I'm looking forward to Bedford. This old place is way too big even for two people. I can be quite independent in my granny flat, and I'll be able to watch my grandchildren grow up. It'll be lovely.'

'But your friends here—'

'I can email, phone, and visit. I'm not decrepit yet, you know. Now stop talking rubbish and help me fold these sheets.'

Martina felt a huge weight lift from her shoulders. All those weeks she had worried needlessly.∴.

As arranged, Jack and the three children were waiting by the floral clock the following afternoon. Martina smiled and waved as Carol, Al and Zoe ran to meet Evan.

Jack took Martina's arm. 'I can see it's all right,' he murmured. 'You look as if you've come alive overnight.'

Martina nodded, and suddenly he bent and kissed her.

'Yeuch! Stop being so soppy!' Evan's face was a picture, and the other three children were giggling behind their hands.

Martina's gaze met Jack's. He looked as surprised by their kiss as she was.

But somehow, it felt right. This could be special, Martina thought. And it was only the start.

The Cat's Whiskers

It was all Mum's fault.

If she hadn't gone on an extended holiday to sunny California, leaving me in charge of what seemed like half a zoo, I wouldn't have needed a playpen for the kittens. And if I hadn't needed the playpen, I would never have met Lucy... but maybe I should start at the beginning.

The phone call came at the end of May.

'Joe, darling! I'm a grandma! The baby's here, it's a girl, and my flights booked for next week!'

Obviously, I was delighted. My first niece! And Mum's first grandchild. My sister Julie and her husband Stan were in the middle of a three-year stay in the States while Stan finished a degree course, so we couldn't exactly pop round straightaway to admire the new addition to the family. But Mum had planned to spend all summer helping out with the baby, and then later we would both go over and have a Californian Christmas and New Year.

'What can I do?' I asked, after we'd enthused about our new relative.

'Well, um – why don't you come for dinner after work this evening? There's something I need to ask you.'

Was I imagining it, or did she sound a touch cagey?

It was just after six when I arrived at Mum's. I'd left the nest a couple of years ago, and Mum had sold the old family house and moved into the long, semi-detached, ex-farm cottage shortly afterwards. She had a big garden where she kept chickens, the air was as fresh as you could wish, and town was a mere five minutes away by car. It was perfect, which was important, as Mum spent most of her time there, working from home doing freelance secretarial work.

Tonight, the table was set in the dining room, overlooking the flower garden. Mum cut me a large slice of quiche and passed the coleslaw.

'Thing is, Joe darling, Connie next door can't look after things here while I'm away. She'll be in hospital until the end of the week, and then she's going to her daughter's for a while, to recuperate.'

I began to see where we were heading. 'Ah, you want me to look after the hens, and water the plants. No problem,' I said, reaching for the beetroot.

'The hens are going up to the farm,' said Mum. 'Actually, it's Geraldine. She's staying here, so if you could just pop by every day and see that everything's okay…'

I was surprised. Geraldine, Mum's tabby cat, was a sociable being and usually spent her holidays with my cousin Anita in town. I looked at Geraldine, who was lying in the sunshine by the window, a big ball of contentment. A very big ball, actually...

I glanced over at Mum. She was sitting watching me, the ghost of a smile on her face. Terror filled my soul, and I nearly dropped my fork.

'But I don't know the first thing about having kittens!' I wailed.

Mum patted my shoulder. 'Don't worry, darling. Geraldine will do the hard bit. All she'll need is food, water, peace and quiet, and she wouldn't get that at Anita's with Jay and the twins galloping about all over the place.'

Fortunately for me, Geraldine was obliging enough to produce her family of four just two days before Mum's departure. I went round to see them the following evening.

'She's being just splendid. You'll have no trouble at all,' Mum enthused.

I peered at the kittens, ensconced in the bottom drawer of the old-fashioned kitchen dresser, now padded out with an old blanket. Geraldine glared at me ferociously, flexing her claws. I didn't appear to be her number one choice of visitor, and I backed off before she went into attack mode.

However, over the next week or two I had to admit that Mum had been right. It was absolutely no trouble to go by on my way to and from work every day and feed Geraldine and check on the kittens. They were very cute, soft little bundles of fur, all tabbies like their mum. It was hard to tell them apart, except by size and temperament. I gave them names, though I knew it was daft – Mum wouldn't keep all four. There was Charlie, the biggest one, and Baby, the smallest, and as it was virtually impossible to distinguish between the other two, I called them Duke and Wellington, because they had adorable little black paws.

They all grew quickly, and soon their eyes were open and they began to explore their surroundings. And that was when the problems started...

The dresser drawer was comfortably padded, but it was a good few inches above floor level and I began to be afraid that Charlie would fall out one day. He seemed to be drawn irresistibly to the edge of the drawer, and would try his little hardest to get up and over the top. Geraldine stopped him quickly enough if she was there, but nowadays she didn't spend every single second with her babies – and of course, it was at exactly those times that Charlie made his most determined efforts to escape.

I emailed Mum in California for advice, but she wasn't able to offer much help. *Look for a big box, or something*, she emailed back. *There might be one in the shed*.

She'd attached the latest photos of baby Kirsten and the family, and I examined them eagerly. The baby looked like a baby, Mum looked like the original Cheshire Cat, and my sister looked as if someone had given her the moon. Suddenly, I felt lonely. Every single one of my near family was in California, and I was home alone.

Geraldine gave a miaow of alarm and pulled Charlie back from the edge of the drawer. I stood up briskly. Geraldine and *her* family needed my attention right now.

I didn't know it then, but that was the most important day of my life.

There I was, banging around in the shed, looking for a suitable box, when I became aware of a head peering round the doorway. An absolutely gorgeous head with dark blonde hair and a worried expression.

'Oh,' she said. 'I heard a noise and I thought maybe a fox had got stuck in here so I came to have a look. Is everything okay?'

I abandoned my search and dusted myself down. 'Sort of. I'm Joe Dawson – I guess you must be Connie's daughter?' She could only have come from next door; there was nowhere else within half a mile.

She nodded. 'I'm just collecting some stuff for Mum. She's being discharged to my sister's tomorrow. I'm Lucy Aitken.'

I grinned at her. 'You don't happen to have a large box floating around, do you?' I explained about Geraldine and the kits, and of course she wanted to go in to see them.

'Oh!' she exclaimed, dropping to her knees beside the dresser drawer and rescuing Baby from under Duke – or Wellington. 'Aren't they gorgeous? How old are they?'

'Just over three weeks.' All at once I was aware

that here was the girl I was going to fall in love with for ever and ever. She was so perfect, and she was looking at me with a very strange expression on her face, too. The air was positively tingling, but at that moment Charlie made yet another bid for freedom and actually did fall out of the drawer this time.

'Charlie, darling!' Lucy scooped him up and kissed his nose, and I realised I was jealous of a three-week-old kitten. Murmuring endearments, Lucy deposited Charlie back beside Geraldine, who was purring placidly. Obviously, Lucy rated higher than I did. A girl thing, maybe. I swallowed. Geraldine was right – Lucy was the best thing ever...

She rubbed behind Charlie's ears, then jumped to her feet and grinned at me. 'I've got just the thing for you in the car,' she announced. 'It's supposed to be going to a car boot sale at the weekend, so you're in luck.'

She raced off and returned a few minutes later with a wooden playpen which she proceeded to erect in Mum's kitchen. She was right, it was just the thing. We wove a couple of sheets through the bars to make side walls, and soon had the whole contraption Charlie-proofed. Lucy positioned kitchen chairs beside and in the playpen to make it easier for Geraldine to get in and out, and we moved the cat family into their new quarters. And it seemed so right, here in the kitchen with Lucy, working together...

The kittens started to explore, and Geraldine settled down in the corner with a 'thank goodness for that' expression on her face. I was just working up the courage to ask Lucy out for a drink, or a walk by the river, or anything, really, when she dropped a bombshell and all my tentative hopes and dreams vanished.

'I should go,' she said, rinsing her hands at the sink. 'I've to take Mum's case to the hospital now, and then I'll need to get packing myself – I'm off to Crete for two weeks tomorrow.' She looked at me, and her expression was an odd mixture of regret and something else – was it hope? Or was she simply looking forward to her holiday? It was difficult to tell, and impossible to ask.

Disappointment pierced right through me. 'Lucky you,' I managed. 'Crete's fantastic.'

She nodded and for a moment we stood staring at each other. The air was tingling again – or was it only tingling for me? And what could I say, anyway? Please don't go, I think I love you... that seemed more than a bit melodramatic. And somehow, the right words just wouldn't come.

And then she was gone, and the very next instant I realised what I should have said and done. It would have been the most natural thing in the world, surely, to ask for a phone number to send on a couple of photos of the kittens as they grew? But no, I had simply let her go, without doing anything to show her that she was the only woman on earth for me. What an idiot I was.

On the other hand, for all I knew she was already in a relationship, and off for a lovely romantic holiday in the sun. But no, surely not... She had looked at me with that expression; there *had* been something there – hadn't there? But maybe not. Lucy was gone.

The day had changed from the best in my life to the worst, just like that.

Over the next two weeks, Lucy's visit took on an almost dreamlike quality in my memory. I'd spent less than an hour in her company, but she was still the first thing I thought of when I woke in the morning, and I fell asleep each night wishing with all my heart that she was part of my life.

'Joe, you look like a lovesick spaniel,' our secretary said one day. Tact had never been Jane's strong point.

I sighed, and told her about meeting Lucy and then losing her again.

'Oh, you can fall in love in ten seconds,' she said cheerfully. 'So what are you going to do about it?'

Her remark set me thinking. There hadn't been much I could do with Lucy on Crete, but she'd be home by the end of the week. So – I could either forget about her (impossible) and go around like a lovesick spaniel for the rest of my days, or, I could at least find out if Lucy was attached – and if she wasn't, if she might be interested in becoming attached to me. All I had to do was get hold of her phone number.

Connie's mobile number was in Mum's landline, so that evening I fed the kits, who were jumping all over the place by this time, and sat in the kitchen to make my call.

Connie sounded rather distant, and I couldn't blame her. She probably spent half her life fending off phone calls from young men interested in her youngest daughter. If I hadn't been her neighbour's son, I would probably have been fobbed off with an excuse. But fortunately, I wasn't quite a stranger.

'I'll give you her number, shall I?' she said. 'Then you can get in touch when she's home. They land at about six on Friday.'

They land. Oh, the pain of two little words – and impossible to ask who the other half of 'they' was. My hands were shaking as I noted Lucy's number and thanked Connie. I turned back to the kittens to calm myself down. Charlie, Duke (who was now the second biggest) and Wellington had worked out how to escape from the playpen and would spend most of their time exploring the kitchen now, leaving poor Baby to miaow plaintively all by herself behind bars. It was time to free her.

Glumly, I dismantled the playpen and made up the kittens' bed back in the dresser drawer, which they could all get in and out of quite easily now. Wellington and Charlie started chasing around after a ping-pong ball, but even their antics couldn't cheer me up today. Lucy was on holiday with someone else. Was that someone a friend – or a boyfriend? Did I even have any right to know?

After lunch on Friday I sat in the park staring at my phone. A quick text might be best. I didn't think I could stand actually hearing Lucy's lovely voice telling me that she and her boyfriend had had a brilliant holiday.

I texted quickly. *Hope u had fun. Playpen redundant. Do u want it back? Joe.* I sent it quickly before I could think too hard and get cold feet.

My phone remained silent all afternoon – at least, several people got in touch, but none of them were Lucy. Of course, she'd be in the plane now. Maybe her phone was off. Or maybe – maybe she didn't want the playpen and she didn't want me, either.

I was late going to feed the kits that night. On Fridays a crowd of us went for a drink after work, and if I checked my phone once I must have checked it a hundred times while we were sitting in the little courtyard behind the Black Stallion. I saw Jane looking at me, and left soon after. I didn't need to be told that I still looked like a lovesick spaniel. Today, I even felt like one.

The kittens were alone in the kitchen and clamoured around my feet as I got their grub ready. Geraldine arrived through the cat flap while her family were still eating and I fed her, too. By now I had given up on my mobile and I'd never felt sorrier for myself. It was dire.

I pulled out my phone to take a photo of the kits to send to Mum, and was aiming it at Baby when it buzzed in my hand. My heart started to beat like an express train when I saw the text from Lucy. *Crete super but poor Celia broke her wrist. Will collect playpen at 11 2morrow if OK? Hope you are good.* ☺

I stared at the text for ages, feeling my grin grow until it was stretching from one ear to the other. Lucy had been on Crete with 'poor Celia'. And my gut feeling that there was something special between us was surely right, because everything in Mum's kitchen was rose-coloured now.

Wonderful visions floated through my head: me and Lucy in a lovely country cottage, one with hens in the garden and a cat flap for Charlie, or Wellington, or even all four kits... Well, a man can dream, can't he? And – an eleven o'clock date to collect the playpen might quite possibly turn into a lunch date. In fact, I would just make sure of that now.

I texted back. *OK. Lunch afterwards?*

The answer arrived in ten seconds, and that was when I knew what a million dollars felt like, even though Lucy hadn't written a single word – just – ☺!

All the Difference in the World

Felicity stared at the contents of the parcel and swallowed hard. It wasn't a very tactful present, but then Great-aunt Connie had never been famous for her tact. Lips trembling, Felicity examined the album. *My Family Tree* was printed on the front, in swirling silvery letters. Inside, there were loose-leaf pages for every generation – which was fine, until the last two sections. *My Children*, and *My Grandchildren*.

Two tears ran down Felicity's cheeks, and she dropped the album back into its box. Just three months ago she had learned she would never have children of her own. At twenty-six, she was going to be the last of her family.

'Morning coffee for the birthday lady.' Ross opened the living room door with one foot and edged through with a laden tray. 'And chocolate digestives, and because it's your birthday you get real sugar too. Hey – what's the matter?'

He put the tray on the coffee table and sat beside her, and for a moment Felicity leaned on him, wishing she could share his happiness in the day. Somehow, the news of their prospective childlessness hadn't shaken Ross in quite the same way. But Felicity knew, without a family of her own, her life would always feel incomplete.

'Aunt Connie's sent a family tree album. Look.' She sipped her coffee and watched as Ross leafed through the pages.

'Great – I remember you and your dad trying to sort out his family last time he was here. You could make family diagrams online, and – oh.'

He had come to the back pages.

'Yes, 'oh' is the only thing to say, isn't it?' Felicity wiped her eyes. 'It's silly little things like this that still hurt so much, Ross. Like walking past nappies in the supermarket, and it hits me all over again that I'll never have a baby of my own.'

Ross covered her hand with his own and squeezed hard. 'We're both still getting over the shock. Give it time, Fee. And one day, we'll have to think about adoption. But don't let this poor album ruin your day. Saturday birthdays don't come every year, you know.'

Seeing her husband's boyish, excited face, Felicity pulled herself together. She wanted them to enjoy the day.

Later that week she poured out her feelings on the phone to her dad. They were especially close after losing Felicity's mother four years ago, and he more than anyone – except Ross, of course – had supported her through the first weeks after the diagnosis. Though come to think of it, Aunt Connie had been very supportive too...

'That's odd.' John Stark's voice sounded considerably nearer than three hundred miles away, and Felicity felt herself relax. 'I can only think Connie didn't notice the back pages. But that's not like her either.'

'I know. I think I'll go and visit her. She must have a reason for wanting me to do the family tree, and she could help with Mum's side of the family. Could you send me all those old certificates and papers – and any old photos you can spare?'

'Of course. I'm glad you're taking the job in hand.'

In spite of the ache in her heart, Felicity tackled the family tree album with her usual energy. She found an ancestor-hunting website, and emailed for details. It was strange how thinking about her great-grandparents gave her such a sense of peace. James and Emily, who gave birth to Sarah... and here, today, was Felicity.

It was the following weekend when things came to a head. On Sunday afternoon, Felicity and Ross set out to walk to Farnam Park, a nearby beauty spot with a lake at one end and the remains of an abbey at the other. Ross had proposed by the lakeside, and since then they'd returned often.

'Oh, I do love it here.' Felicity dropped down on the springy grass and gazed over the water to the woods on the far side. 'It's so peaceful.'

'Mm. Not even many hikers today. Look – look! There's a fox, just coming out of the woods! See it?'

Felicity watched as the fox stood motionless for a few seconds, then trotted along the edge of the wood. Three little cubs followed on, gamboling briefly in the sunlight before they all disappeared back into the dimness under the trees. Felicity sat there frozen, not looking at Ross. Even here, in the middle of nowhere, she was confronted by mothers and babies.

After a while Ross turned to her. 'Let's talk, Fee. We can't spend our lives avoiding babies and feeling awkward every time a family of fox cubs turns up. You know we both want children – so we have to think about adoption.'

Felicity picked a long piece of grass and twirled it between her finger and thumb. 'I wanted *our* child.' Her voice was trembling. 'You know that.'

He hugged her. 'I know – so did I. But darling, don't you think that if we adopt a baby, we would love it just as much? I think it would become our child very quickly.'

Felicity nodded slowly. 'You could be right,' she admitted. 'But we might not get a baby, you know. It might be an older child. We might have to wait for years. And–'

'Stop it!' Ross pulled away from her and Felicity jumped in fright. 'Fee, *we can't* have our own baby. So will you please stop thinking about an adopted child as second best? It's first best for us.'

He leapt up and strode off along the lakeside, but not before Felicity had seen the tears in his eyes. Horrified, she scrambled up and ran after him.

'Ross! I'm sorry. You're right. We'll phone the

agency first thing tomorrow.'

At nine the next morning, Felicity lifted the phone. She had spent the previous evening reading her way through various adoption websites and gathering as much information as she could.

The woman who answered was pleasant and reassuring. She would email an application form, and more information, and an agency worker would be in touch as soon as their application had been checked.

'Well, yes,' she said, in answer to Felicity's question. 'It can take longer than nine months to adopt, and it isn't often a tiny baby, either. But my colleague will explain all that when she sees you.'

Felicity ended the call with a feeling of relief. She had taken the first step towards a child of their own.

That evening, she tackled the pile of certificates and photos her dad had sent. She started to separate them out, but quickly realised that most of the certificates were from her dad's side.

'It's odd,' she said to Ross, who was flicking through a travel book. 'There's next to nothing about my grandmother here. Just these baptismal certificates for Gran and her sisters, Connie and Olivia.'

The three certificates were fragile and yellowed. Felicity stared for a moment before she realised what was puzzling her. Gran – Rachel – was two years older than her sister Olivia and four years older than Connie, but Connie had been baptised first. And Rachel and Olivia were baptised on the same day...

'I must visit Aunt Connie soon,' she said. 'It's a real mystery.'

Thing were hectic for the next few days. Felicity's boss was off sick, and Ross, with a streaming cold, was very sorry for himself and kept her busy producing hot drinks. Felicity had no time even to think about family trees.

On Thursday evening, the adoption agency worker came. After nearly two hours of questions and discussion, Mrs Workman nodded.

'That's enough for just now,' she said, packing her papers together. 'But as you don't seem to have any terrible skeletons in the closet, we can move things along as quickly as possible. Your homework for next time is what we mentioned before – think about whether you could offer a home to an older child, or one from a different ethnic background, or a handicapped child. Would a week on Tuesday suit you both for the next meeting? After that, you'd start the preparation classes.'

'Well – she's given us plenty to think about,' said Ross, as Mrs Workman's car disappeared round the corner. 'Let's treat ourselves to a weekend away to talk it through. We could go to the Yorkshire Moors and do some walking – and visit Aunt Connie on the way.'

Felicity beamed. She felt as if an enormous weight had been lifted from her shoulders. Their child was going to happen. 'Great. You know, I'm glad now Aunt

Connie gave me that album. It gave me a shove and got things moving. I can't wait to start on the *My Children* page!'

Great-aunt Connie lived in Ilkley, in an attractive sheltered housing complex. She opened the door with her usual big smile.

'Come through to the sitting room; I've made coffee. I know you can't stay long, but I do want to know how you're getting on with the family tree, Fee.'

There was a roguish twinkle in Aunt Connie's eye, and Felicity stared. 'Auntie, what are you up to? You know something! Tell me – what's all this with the baptismal certificates Dad sent me? Why were you baptised first?'

Aunt Connie poured out coffee and handed round ginger biscuits. 'You are slow, Fee,' she said cheerfully. Haven't you guessed? Rachel, Olivia and I were all adopted. My mother couldn't have her own. Just like you. It was different in those days; no-one talked about that kind of thing, not even in the family. But they adopted me as a baby, and Rachel and Olivia two years later. They were sisters, four and six at the time. Later, none of us could remember the time when we *weren't* sisters. And I know my parents truly felt they had three daughters of their own.'

Felicity glanced at Ross, then got up to hug her great-aunt. 'Thank you, Auntie,' she said chokily. 'That's made all the difference in the world.'

Great-aunt Connie's ninety-fifth birthday party was a big family occasion. Seven-year-old Oliver had never seen so many balloons tied to an apple tree.

'Mum said we can take some home,' he informed his sister. 'I'll have seven, and you can have three. And Sarah can have two, though she's not quite two yet.'

Hannah's lower lip trembled. 'I want seven too,' she said. 'Mummy, I want seven balloons too – please?'

Felicity looked down at the little girl and laughed. 'Oh, you can all have seven balloons,' she said happily. She cuddled sleepy Sarah and watched Oliver pull Hannah towards the tree. How very blessed they were. Three wonderful children – *her* children, though she hadn't known it. They'd had Olly for five years now, and Hannah and Sarah for almost two. How lucky they were...

Suddenly her son was beside her again.

'Mummy,' he said anxiously, tugging at her sleeve. 'There's three of us, you know. Will we have room for twenty-one balloons in the car?'

Speedy to the Rescue!

Marion Banks stepped out onto the decking, and bent to snap a couple of dead heads off the pansies in her wooden tub before straightening up and glancing at the sky. Cloudless. She would have half an hour in the vegetable plot – the weeds were gaining the upper hand.

She was busy hoeing around the potato plants when the landline shrilled out from the living room, and for a moment she stood still, listening. Davy would get that; he'd been knee-deep in his Sudoku book when she'd left him. But the phone rang on.

Marion dropped her hoe and jogged inside. What on earth was Davy doing? The living room was deserted, and she snatched up the phone.

'Hello?' Marion sank down on an armchair, grinning ruefully when she saw Davy outside on the street, rubbing the car with a tattered chamois leather. That car had been polished to within an inch of its life nearly every day since Davy had retired. Oh, he had plenty of outside interests, and he'd done all the right things, planning and preparing for retirement – but there was still a lot of day to get through.

'Oh good – you are in,' said a familiar voice in Marion's ear.

She laughed. 'Morning, Doris. How's life at your end?'

'We're having a bit of an emergency,' said her friend. 'You know we planned a week in Italy? The hiking holiday?'

'Yes – you go on Wednesday, don't you?' said Marion apprehensively. Doris had been looking forward to her trip for weeks, surely nothing had happened to spoil the holiday.

'That's the idea. The problem is, I thought Jim had booked Bingo into the kennels and he thought I'd done it, and we only discovered last night that neither of us had. I called them a few minutes ago – we've been using them for years and I thought they'd maybe squeeze poor Bingo in even without a booking, but they're in the middle of renovating the place and they're not taking holiday dogs at the moment...'

Marion laughed again. 'Doris, it will be a pleasure to look after Bingo, don't worry. Davy's home all day now and Bingo's a lamb – or he would be if he wasn't a Dalmatian! I've been trying to persuade Davy to get a dog, but he's never had one and you know him, he takes forever and a day to get used to a new idea. Bingo might be just what we need.'

Pleased, she rang off and went to tell Davy about their holiday guest.

The following Friday afternoon saw Marion and Davy, well wrapped-up against a brisk north wind, striding towards the common behind town, Bingo trotting along on his lead beside them. Davy had been sceptical when he'd first heard about the dog-sitting, but Marion was glad to see him look more enthusiastic as each day passed. As soon as they reached the grass, he clicked the lead off and started a game of fetch with Bingo's favourite ball. The dog's grin as he hurtled after the ball was a joy to see, and Marion found herself grinning too, in spite of the cold.

They were heading home back across the common when a little black and tan dog with big ears rushed up to make friends with Bingo. Marion looked around for a dog-less owner, but there was no one to be seen. They stopped for a moment, uncertain what to do.

'Shoo!' Marion said to the little dog. 'Home! Good boy!'

The dog looked up at her, panting, and she noticed there was no identity disc on his collar.

'Maybe he's a stray.'

Davy shrugged. 'Doubt it. You don't often see stray dogs around here. He's probably just lost. What is he, anyway?'

'I think he's a Manchester terrier. Mum's neighbour used to have one. Oh, dear – what should we do?'

They walked to the edge of the common, the terrier racing round them all the way. There was still no sign of a worried owner, and Davy and Marion looked at each other.

'Let's phone the kennels,' said Marion eventually. 'That's the first place anyone would ask if they'd lost a dog, and Doris said they were still open for strays. Maybe he's got one of those chips implanted.'

She crouched down and held out her hand to the terrier, who sniffed cautiously. Marion looped her scarf – what a good thing she was wearing her long one! – through his collar.

'Come on, Speedy, my lad!' she said, gripping the ends of the scarf. 'Let's see if we can find where you belong!'

Gemma Donaldson gave the food preparation table a last wipe and looked round, satisfied. The dogs were all fed, and Colin and Joanne were seeing to the cats today. Soon it would be time to let the dogs out for a sniff around the yard, and then she would be off duty until Sunday.

Gemma wandered along to the main office, looking in on the new little terrier as she passed. He was fast asleep on his blanket in the 'new arrivals' section, and Gemma smiled. Surely someone would claim him soon; he was obviously well looked-after.

Colin and Joanne were laughing and joking together as Gemma passed them in the yard, and she felt a sudden stab of envy. They'd had their engagement party just last week. How lucky they were, and how very much she would love to find someone special to share her life with. But here she was, nearly twenty-three, and there was no one at all in her life at the moment, never mind anyone special.

Sam, the manager, was on the phone when she went into the office, a frown on his normally cheerful face. He clattered the receiver down and turned to Gemma.

'Problem. A family of six pups plus mum are coming in. If we take them – and it seems they've been abandoned so we really have to – there's no room any more for the terrier that was brought in earlier. I wish these renovations were over and done with. It's a real pain being squeezed into half the building like this.'

Gemma nodded. 'Never mind, only another three weeks to go. It'll be worth all the hassle when it's done.'

She was about to leave Sam to cope with the dog problem when Colin and Joanne arrived with Robbie, the new team member. Gemma sighed. Robbie was a lovely guy, but unfortunately he didn't seem interested in her. The nice guys were always taken; it was the story of her life.

'Can anyone look after a terrier over the weekend?' said Sam. 'Nice dog, unofficially named Speedy, found wandering on the common today so he might be claimed quite quickly.'

Gemma shook her head. 'I'm helping a friend choose her wedding dress so I'll be out all day tomorrow.' Another wedding where she wouldn't have a partner. It was a lonely feeling.

Colin and Joanne were shaking their heads too, and Sam turned to Robbie.

'I can't take him myself,' said Robbie slowly. 'But my sister might. She stopped work last week – she's expecting twins in eight weeks – so she'd have time. She loves dogs.'

Ten minutes later, Gemma brought the terrier round to the office where Robbie was completing the paperwork for it to go to his sister's. Speedy was delighted to be out of his box, and greeted Robbie enthusiastically.

Gemma laughed. 'He's so friendly, isn't he? I wonder how he managed to get lost like this. He just loves people.'

Robbie nodded, and she saw that his face was flushed.

'Yes… um, Gemma – could you maybe help me take him to my sister's?'

Gemma stared. Transporting a small dog across town – especially a friendly one like Speedy – wasn't a two-man job, even for a new person. Robbie's face was almost magenta now, and suddenly Gemma understood. He was shy. And now he was asking her to go somewhere with him. Maybe he did like her, after all…

'I'd love to!' She put as much warmth as possible into her voice, and he beamed.

'Let's go, then. Um… there's a new coffee bar near my sister's place, maybe…'

'Why don't we try it out when we've dropped Speedy off?' Gemma hugged herself as his face lit up again. 'Thanks, Speedy,' she whispered, bending to pat the dog's sleek black head.

Kate Docherty smiled as Speedy appeared in the kitchen doorway.

'You've had your grub, young man. This is my lunch. But afterwards we'll go for a lovely walk in the park. You'll enjoy that.'

She settled down on the sofa with her sandwich and a glass of orange juice. Speedy went back to his blanket in the corner, though Kate was amused to see his eyes watching her every bite. She was glad of his company, anyway; she'd felt distinctly down after finishing work, and with Graeme on a business trip she was home alone all week now. Of course, it was great to have time to relax and get things organised for the babies, but what with only moving here in March and working full-time, she didn't know many people in the area yet.

After her rest, she looked round for Speedy's lead and set off towards the park, the little dog running along at her side. They'd had a good walk yesterday too, with Robbie and the girl he worked with. Kate smiled to herself. She'd seen the expression on Robbie's face when he looked at Gemma. It would be great if she and Robbie got together properly.

But today it was just her and Speedy. Kate walked round the duck pond, passing several little groups of young women with buggies, chatting together and watching older children on the swings. She would do that one day too, when the babies were older, but right now she didn't know anyone to chat to... Lonely tears welled up in Kate's eyes as she walked towards the park gate and home.

A football whizzing past her left ear made her stumble. Speedy barked, jerking the lead as he tried to race after the ball, and Kate struggled to keep her balance. A young woman rushed over and grabbed her elbow.

'Kevin and Paul, you just take that ball back to the football pitch,' she said, waving a couple of small boys away and turning to Kate, a concerned look on her face. 'Are you all right?'

'I'm fine,' said Kate, gripping Speedy's lead more firmly. The young woman stepped back to her abandoned buggy, where a rosy-cheeked toddler was gazing at her with big eyes. Kate smiled at the child, a lump in her throat. Soon now she would have her own babies to push around the park, oh, how good it was going to be.

'I'm Julie. I haven't seen you here before – is that your first?' Julie nodded towards Kate's bump.

'And second. It's twins. Eight weeks to go. How old is your little one?'

'One next Saturday. Hey, why don't we go for a cup of something and a chat? There's a café on the High Street with tables outside.'

Later that afternoon Kate arrived back home feeling she had made a friend and put down another little root in town. She patted Speedy, who was sniffing hopefully in his bowl.

'Well, it's thanks to you that I went to the park today, and I'm very glad I did,' she told him. 'You can have an extra piece of sausage tonight, Speedy.' She sank down on the sofa and smiled. Tomorrow, Julie and little Bethany were coming to visit, and she was invited to Beth's birthday party too. She'd meet more young mums there. And next week Graeme would be home again and she could introduce him to her new friends. All at once, life seemed a lot less lonely.

'Here you are, love.' Marion put a mug of coffee on the small table by Davy's chair. 'You're looking glum today – did you get the lawnmower fixed?'

'Yes. It needed a new spark plug, like I thought.' Davy sipped his coffee and bent to pat Bingo, who was lying at his feet as usual. Marion watched, amused. Bingo so obviously thought Davy was the bee's knees, and the feeling appeared to be mutual. Maybe her dream of having a dog of their own would come true sooner rather than later. Doris and Jim were coming this evening to collect Bingo, so now might be a good time... But Davy got there first.

'I've been thinking,' he said, leaning towards Marion. 'I could give the kennels a ring and ask what's happening with that little Speedy. See if anyone's claimed him. I've got used to having a dog about the place, and I know you've wanted one for ages.'

Marion nodded, wondering if she should mention the litter of Labradors she'd heard of at the weekend. Wait and see what happens, she told herself. A smaller, older dog like Speedy would actually suit them better than a pup.

Davy checked the kennel's website and lifted the phone. Marion sat listening as he spoke.

'...the little terrier we brought in last week... Yes... If no one has claimed him we could offer him a home here... I see... Oh, dear... I'll do that. Thank you very much.'

He put the phone down and grinned at Marion, who was watching apprehensively. It hadn't sounded like good news from where she was sitting.

'They heard yesterday that Speedy belonged to an elderly man who moved to Canada to live with his family there. Speedy went to a neighbour, but he didn't get on with their cat and he ran away. Imagine, he's come all the way from Dunbank! Anyway, he's up for adoption and we can go tomorrow and do the paperwork if we want him!' A huge grin split his face.

Just after ten the next morning they were parking outside the kennels. Davy was like a dog himself, thought Marion – one with two tails! The paperwork was quickly seen to, and Marion looked round hopefully when the young woman they'd seen the last time came into the room. She was alone, though.

'Could you possibly collect Speedy this afternoon? He's staying with my colleague's sister in Glenburn,' she explained apologetically. 'Robbie was supposed to pick him up for you, but his car's broken down.'

'Can't we just fetch him up ourselves?' suggested Marion. 'We live in Glenburn too, so he must be practically on our way home.'

As it turned out, Speedy was staying just a few streets away from Marion and Davy's home. A small, pretty, and very pregnant young woman opened the door when they rang the bell. Speedy was careering about at her feet, and rushed to welcome Marion and Davy.

'See, he remembers us!' said Davy, and the young woman smiled.

It was a friendly smile, thought Marion, but the poor girl was clearly exhausted, and Gemma had said she was on her own this week...

'Kate, isn't it? Why don't we let Davy and Speedy go for a walk now, and, um, you and I could have a cup of tea while you tell me about Speedy's routine?' suggested Marion tactfully.

Kate's face brightened. 'That would be lovely. I haven't slept well the past couple of nights so I'm too tired to go out much, but all this time indoors is driving me nuts! Some company would be fantastic.'

Ten minutes later Marion had heard the whole story about the twins and Graeme's business trip and Kate making friends with Julie – and also the fact that there were no grandparents around to help out.

'That's settled, then,' she said. 'You've got yourself an honorary grandma and grandpa for your babies – if you'll have us. Why don't you finish your tea now and go for a sleep, and then tonight Davy can pick you up and bring you to us for dinner. That way, Speedy won't feel quite so unsettled,' she added diplomatically, pleased when Kate nodded.

Late that evening, Marion checked the locks before going to bed. Speedy was fast asleep in his new basket, snoring gently.

'Well, my lad, you've changed a few people's lives this week,' she said softly. 'We've all got more friends

now, thanks to you!'
And Speedy snored on...

After Rebecca

I didn't realise it at the time, but meeting Rebecca was the most important thing that had ever happened to me. That chance encounter split my life into two distinct parts – before Rebecca, and after.

A lot had happened in our family that summer. George, my older brother, married and went to work in the States for a year, and my sister Amanda announced that baby number one would be arriving in September. Mum and Dad were over the moon, of course – first grandchild and all that – but I was glad to leave the marriage and children to my siblings. After last year's debacle when Michael, my boyfriend since fifth year at school, had walked away with barely a backward glance, I was off men. Big time.

September came, and with it baby Neil, my degree, and a fabulous job in the university archives. I settled down to enjoy life as part of the working world, and started saving for a trip to visit George and Annie. Mum and Dad were revelling in their new grandparenthood, of course, and I helped them pack the car with lovingly knitted baby clothes and the antique family cradle, and waved them off on an extended visit to Amanda's.

So there I was, in sole charge of the house, and that was when the really important thing happened. I met Rebecca.

It was one of those glorious September afternoons, not quite summer, not quite autumn, but with all the advantages of both. I had the day off to compensate for working the previous weekend, and I went for lunch with an old school friend. We indulged in some retail therapy afterwards and I found a gorgeous black skirt, so I was quite pleased with my day when I arrived back home. Coffee mug in hand, I'd just put my feet up when the doorbell rang.

'My dad's not at home and neither is Mrs Bradshaw or the Wilsons or Mr and Mrs Cameron,' announced the miniature, blue-uniformed figure on the doorstep.

I'd seen her before; she had moved into the house at the bottom of the lane two or three weeks ago, but I'd never actually spoken to any of the family.

'Oh,' I said, somewhat nonplussed. 'You'd better come in, then. Who brought you home from school?'

'Tilly's mum, because I go there to play after school till my dad collects me on his way home from work. But today she brought me straight home because they're going to the dentist and she just dropped me off at the gate because she was running late as usual,' the child explained, panting slightly, dark blonde hair escaping from the blue Alice band around her head. 'My dad said he would be home but he's not so I went to Mrs Bradshaw's and—'

'Yes, I see.' I interrupted the list of all the neighbours between our two houses and led her into the kitchen. 'I'm Stacie. What's your name?'

'Rebecca Susanna Granger – and I'm five,' she said, depositing her school rucksack beside the table and looking round the kitchen, which I'll admit wasn't as tidy as Mum would have liked.

I opened the fridge. 'Have some orange juice, and then we'll go and see if your dad's back. Or do you have a phone number for him? And what about your mum?'

Rebecca shook her head. 'Mummy lives in Paris with Phillippe – he's my step-dad,' she said matter-of-factly. 'She travels a lot for her job so I live with my dad and sometimes I go to Mummy's in the holidays, but mostly I stay with my dad and I don't have a phone of my own because my dad says I'm not big enough yet.'

I supplied her with a glass of juice which she polished off in about ten seconds while I gulped down the rest of my coffee. It occurred to me that her father might have arrived home in the meantime and be frantically searching for his child, but when we arrived at their place there was no sign of his car, and the door was still locked.

Rebecca's lip trembled. 'He said he would be home. He's always home when he says he is.' Her voice was wobbling dangerously.

I put an arm round her. Poor little thing; she had moved from goodness knows where to a new house and probably started a new school, all without a mum, and now she had mislaid her dad.

'Never mind, Rebecca.' I fished in my handbag. 'Look, we'll put a note on the door to say you're with me, and then you can keep me company for a little while until your dad gets home. My mum and dad have left me alone here too, you know. They've gone to help my sister with her baby.'

Back home, the photos of baby Neil which Mum had emailed kept Rebecca distracted for quite a long time. We were clicking through the collection for the second time when the thought struck me that her father was quite seriously late now. Had he phoned one of their immediate neighbours in the meantime? I left Rebecca at the kitchen table with the laptop, and went to do some phoning of my own. No one had heard anything from Rebecca's father, but I learned that his name was Joseph and he was a violinist with the town's symphony orchestra. I sniffed. A woolly-headed musician who had forgotten all about his daughter, no doubt. Or forgotten the time and Tilly's dental appointment, anyway. Mrs Bradshaw offered to take Rebecca, but I was quite happy looking after her. I'd never had anything to do with children that age, and she was a bright, interesting little thing.

'When I have a baby I'm going to look after it all the time, and I'm going to make cakes with it and play with it and collect it from school and buy it pretty dresses, and I'm going to sing to it every night before it goes to sleep,' she announced, turning away from the last picture of baby Neil. 'Aren't you, Stacie?'

A huge lump came into my throat as she spoke. What a love she was. Was all that a list of what she missed about not living with her mother? I stroked her head.

'Absolutely,' I said. 'Men are rubbish at making cakes, aren't they?'

'My dad is,' she said, beaming suddenly. 'When I was five he tried to make a birthday cake but when it came out the tin it looked more like a ski slope than a cake, my dad said, so we made trifle with it and he bought me a cake with five candles and a pink ribbon instead. My dad says shop cakes are cool, but I'd like to make icing in a bowl and then scrape it out afterwards and lick the spoon and make it all different colours too, like Tilly and her mum did last week when Tilly was five and she had a blue and green cake with—'

The doorbell interrupted her and we both dashed through to the hallway. I was fully expecting to see a contrite and woolly musician on the doorstep, but much to my dismay, two uniformed police officers were standing there.

'No need to worry, everything's okay,' the older of the two said immediately, eying Rebecca.

He was holding the note I'd stuck to Joseph Granger's front door. I introduced myself and Rebecca, and invited them through to the kitchen. Rebecca was clinging to me now, her eyes wide and her face pale.

I took her on my lap. The older policeman told us that Rebecca's dad had collapsed in the supermarket earlier that afternoon, presumably on his way home, and been taken to hospital where they'd diagnosed acute appendicitis and promptly operated. It was only when he came out of the anaesthetic afterwards that Joseph remembered Tilly's visit to the dentist and the fact that Rebecca wasn't going there after school today.

'So we came straight here to find you,' said the older policeman, smiling kindly at Rebecca, who was blinking hard.

'I want to go to my dad,' she whispered.

I rubbed her back. 'I'll take you right away. Off you go and wash your face first.' I bundled her into the downstairs loo and returned to the policemen in the kitchen. 'Is it really all right?'

Both men nodded. 'She'll need a place to stay for a couple of nights, but her dad said he can arrange that,' the older policeman said. 'We'll let the hospital know that Rebecca's fine and you're on your way.'

I collected my handbag and car key, combed Rebecca's hair and my own, and off we set. Rebecca was silent in the back for most of the journey. When we stopped at the traffic lights by the station I turned to reassure her again.

'Appendicitis isn't a big deal nowadays, sweetie. It's a very quick operation and most folk only have to stay in hospital for a day or two afterwards. Your dad might feel a bit woozy tonight, you know, after the injection that makes you go to sleep while the doctors are doing the operation. But you really don't have to worry, Rebecca.'

I was sorry I'd said that when I saw Joe Granger. He was alone in a side room and he looked terrible, dark shadows under his eyes and a throaty voice from the anaesthetic.

'I'm fine, don't worry,' he croaked, stroking Rebecca's face. She was standing as close as she could get, clutching him for dear life, her dark blonde head matching his on the pillow.

He looked at me pleadingly, brown eyes searching my face for reassurance about his daughter. I could positively feel the love between them.

'Could you arrange for her to stay at Tilly's tonight,' he whispered. 'I might get home tomorrow.'

Personally, I doubted this, but I promised to do the needful for Rebecca. Sister came in and shooed Rebecca and me out, and the tension in Rebecca's little body as she turned in the doorway to wave goodbye was all too apparent.

'He'll look much better tomorrow, darling,' I said as we walked along the pale green hospital corridor, Rebecca with two tears running down her cheeks.

We drove home in silence, and I made hot chocolate for Rebecca and sat down to call Tilly's mum, whose name, according to the phone book, was Caroline Simmons. There was no reply, however, and I made a spot decision.

'Would you like to stay here with me?' I suggested, and Rebecca nodded solemnly. I called the hospital, but Joe was asleep so I left a message. Rebecca and

I walked down the lane to Mrs Bradshaw, who had a key for the Granger home, and we fetched her pyjamas and a few other necessities. The house was untidy, with masses of books everywhere and a beautiful piano in the living room. A fair number of half-full removal boxes were lying around too, and I remembered the Grangers hadn't been here long. Poor Rebecca. It was a lot for a child to cope with.

Fortunately, the next day was Saturday. Rebecca slept until after nine o'clock, and I was glad to see she looked more like the child who'd arrived on my doorstep the day before.

'Do you think my dad will get home today?' She stood watching as I heated lentil soup for lunch. 'Because if he has to stay we could take him some grapes and some books and his iPod with his music, and some juice and his laptop and—'

'We'll see what the sister says.' Amused, I stopped her before she thought of something vital that might be difficult to get hold of. Truth be told, I was enjoying Rebecca's company. She was warm and funny, and needy, and I was helping her. It made me feel warm.

They'd shifted Joe into the main ward, and he was sitting up in bed with a glum face which brightened considerably when Rebecca ran in, clutching a bag with grapes, a newspaper, and Joe's iPod. She hugged him with an incredibly sweet expression, and my eyes promptly filled with tears.

'Hello, chicken!' he said, hugging back. 'Thank

you so much, Stacie. I got hold of Caro this morning. Apparently Tilly had a complicated time at the dentist's yesterday, but enough said about that. Rebecca can go there today, though. I'm afraid they're not letting me home until Monday.'

Rebecca twisted round in his arms to look at me. 'Can't I stay with you, Stacie? I promise I'll be good and I'll help you bake a cake, if you like, and we could play games and sing songs and I could help you with the shopping too, and please, Stacie...' Her face was imploring.

'Of course you can stay,' I said promptly. 'If that's okay?' I looked inquiringly at Joe.

He was staring at his daughter with a bemused expression in his eyes. 'Well – if you're sure.' He turned his gaze on me.

For a moment I felt quite out of balance. I could feel his love for Rebecca. I had no child of my own to love like that, and all at once I felt as if something terribly important was missing in my life – the whole loving partner and child thing. I'd never thought of it as being vital, but now I could see that it was. And this man was obviously a special kind of person, to have brought up a child like Rebecca. Now he was entrusting her to me, and suddenly I wanted to get to know him a whole lot better. But he was waiting for an answer, and I pushed the complicated thoughts away.

'Oh, I'm very sure,' I said, laughing to lighten the moment. 'We'll have a lovely girly time, won't we, Rebecca?'

And we did. We made cupcakes and decorated them within an inch of their lives; we raided Rebecca's home for games and played Junior Monopoly and Mousetrap, we made spaghetti with cream and bacon sauce for a late dinner, and I gave Rebecca a long, smelly bubble bath, after which we spent ages doing each other's hair. I honestly couldn't remember when I'd had such fun on a Saturday night.

The following day she insisted on taking some of the cakes to her father, and stood pondering for ages about what colours he'd prefer and which were the most beautifully decorated. The love was shining from her eyes as she presented them to him, and again it was all I could do to blink my tears back.

Joe was looking much better, and the three of us sat by his bed and chatted about everything under the sun for the entire two hours' visiting time. It was easy talking to him because he liked the same books and films as I did, and we both enjoyed the same cities – especially Vienna. And with Rebecca around there was never a gap in the conversation anyway.

I found myself admiring the way her father dealt with her. He was loving, firm, funny and supportive all at the same time – it was very touching to watch. I was sorry when it was time to go, and I could see Joe was finding it difficult to say goodbye to Rebecca.

'Take care of her, and thanks,' he said, staring up at me and hugging Rebecca tightly.

I could see the tears in his eyes again, and I didn't want to leave him like this. He and Rebecca had touched a place in my heart. Stop being soppy, I told myself sternly. Tomorrow, Joe will be home again and things will get back to normal.

Somehow, though, things being normal wasn't an attractive prospect. I realised that Joe and Rebecca had something very special, and I wanted to be a part of it. But tomorrow there would be no Joe to visit in the hospital, and no Rebecca to look after.

On the way home Rebecca and I stopped at the supermarket and bought supplies for Joe's first few days at home. She assured me that pizza was his favourite meal, so we bought a ready-made base. I made a garlicky tomato sauce and we organised a selection of toppings, too.

'So all you need to do is put the sauce on the base, add the toppings and the cheese, and put it in the oven,' I told Rebecca. 'Your dad will do the oven bit, but he'll maybe need some help with the other things till he's quite better.'

Silent for once, she nodded, smiling dreamily. Her dad was better again.

The next morning I stood at the gate, waving as Tilly's mum drove off with Rebecca plus schoolbag in the back, and then I grabbed my own stuff and went back to the real world. My world. And all day long I was conscious of that special something that was missing in my life. How on earth was it possible that all my plans had turned themselves upside down in the course of a weekend? This time on Friday I'd barely been aware of Joe and Rebecca's existence. Today, all I could think of was a man with warm brown eyes, and a little girl who needed a mum. And I wasn't a part of their world.

The answering machine was blinking away when I got home that evening.

'Hi, Stacie, it's Joe. Could you please drop by when you get this message? If you can. Thanks.'

Rebecca would need the things she had left here, of course. Soberly, I gathered pyjamas and games and other small-girl bits and pieces that were lying around, and took them with me. Today, I was merely the messenger, and I wanted more than that. I wanted to be part of Rebecca's everyday life and I wanted Joe to look at me with eyes full of love, too. But here I was, a mere neighbour. It was gut-wrenching.

Joe led me into the living room. He looked quite fit now, thought there were still faint shadows in the hollow of his cheeks. He grinned at me, and for a second I thought I saw hope in his eyes. My heart started to hammer.

'Stacie, I wanted to thank you for looking after Rebecca so well. I could tell she was really happy with you, in spite of her fright and me being stuck in hospital.'

Bleakness filled my soul. He only wanted to say thank you.

'She's a love,' I said thickly. 'Where is she?'

'She'll be back at six. Brownies after school tonight. Seriously, I can never thank you—'

Something snapped inside me and I felt two tears run down my cheeks. I brushed them away impatiently.

'No. Stop. I should be thanking you. I had such a

great time with her, she's an absolute darling and I loved every single minute so don't you dare thank me. You're so lucky to have her.'

His brown eyes met mine and slowly he reached out and wiped two more tears from my face. 'You know, I think you and Rebecca are very much alike,' he said softly, and half a second later I was standing in his arms.

That was the beginning.

And yesterday was the end of the beginning, when Joe and I were married and Rebecca was the frilliest pink bridesmaid imaginable. At the reception I heard her talking to baby Neil in his buggy.

'I'm staying with our grandma for two weeks now because my dad and my mum are going to America for a honeymoon and then...' Her eyes were dreamy again. 'And then they're coming home!'

Corinna's Big Day

Madge stood by the cradle and looked down at the sleeping baby. Corinna's cheeks were pink, and wispy brown hair had grown to cover most of her head now. As Madge watched, one plump hand moved over the green blanket and a thumb found its way into the baby's mouth.

Madge smiled, and rocked the cradle gently. Oh, to be three months old and able to sleep like that, without a care in the world. And in a lovely old wooden cradle, too. Madge's great-grandfather had made it, and it had been handed down through the family ever since. Countless babies had slept in its warm, reassuring depths. Now it was Corinna's turn.

It was funny how a baby took over the house, thought Madge, as she started to fold the washing. There was the cradle, dominating the living room. And the cot in Madge and Tim's bedroom, and the baby-rocker in the kitchen... the changing table over the bath... the pram in the hallway.

Not to mention the countless little things, squeaky toys and baby clothes and bibs... bottles... the list was endless. And all for someone just turned three months old.

Madge folded a pink Babygro and put it into the basket with a sigh. It was so sweet, and Corinna wouldn't wear it again. Such perfect little outfits, worn for such a short time. Ah, well. Maybe – probably – hopefully, someday, another baby would wear the pink suit.

The front door slammed, and nine-year-old Rory ran into the living room.

'Shh! Corinna's sleeping. How was judo?' Madge abandoned the washing and steered her son into the kitchen.

'I beat Danny!' Rory gulped down a glass of orange juice and started on an apple. 'Where are the others?'

'Becky's gone shopping, and Harry's in the shed fixing the lawnmower.' At twelve and fourteen, her two oldest children were quite independent these days. Madge smiled, remembering when Harry had been three months old. How uncertain she'd been in those days! Things that had seemed like insurmountable problems with Harry were just everyday occurrences with Corinna.

A hungry baby wail sounded in the living room. Rory tossed his apple core into the bin.

'Can I give Corinna her bottle? Please? I won't be able to, tomorrow.'

'Okay,' said Madge. 'Go and entertain her while I get it ready.'

She opened the fridge and took out one of the two bottles of baby milk. Just two bottles left. Tears stung in Madge's eyes as she warmed the milk. How time had flown! And yet it was good, too, this passing of time. Becky was a real friend now; quite a different relationship than with a baby. A baby was all and everything, then it grew into a child who in no time was an independent person. What would Corinna be like at twelve? There was no way to know.

Madge was making lunch when Tim arrived home from his job in the local library. He kissed the back of her neck, reaching for the biscuit tin at the same time.

'Well, love, it's Corinna's big day. Reckon we'll manage this afternoon?'

'I've been thinking about it all morning. Oh, we'll manage; we've done it before. But it doesn't get easier, does it? There'll be tears this time too.' Madge stopped, hearing the tremor in her voice.

'Yes. But — you wouldn't want it to be different, would you?'

No, of course not, Madge thought, peering at the shepherd's pie in the oven. 'Lunch!' she called, and immediately four young faces appeared in the doorway. Becky strapped Corinna into the baby-rocker and pulled it over beside her own chair.

Harry accepted his plate from Madge, then looked at his parents warily. 'I think I'll go to Kev's this afternoon. If that's all right?'

'Of course,' said Madge, and Harry looked relieved.

'Well, I'm staying,' said Becky, her chin in the air.

'Right till the last minute. And then—'

Her voice trembled, and she put down her fork.

'Come on, now,' said Madge, patting the girl's hand. 'It's not easy, but it's for the best. And it's such a happy day for Corinna.'

She tipped the baby's nose with one finger, and Corinna gurgled up at her.

Later, Madge tidied the living room while Tim and Rory cleared the kitchen. She bundled the baby toys into their box and pushed it behind the sofa. Right. Two o'clock. It was time to get ready.

She lifted Corinna and took her to the bathroom, laying her on the changing table. The tiny girl laughed and blew bubbles as Madge undressed and washed her.

'Now you make a big effort and stay clean for the next hour,' said Madge. 'It's your big day, you know.'

She opened the plastic bag and took out Corinna's new clothes. A slightly-too-large yellow cotton vest with matching knickers, and a yellow and white striped baby suit with a lamb on the front. Corinna giggled when Madge brushed the wispy hair. It was so hard. Madge lifted the baby and held her close, fighting back tears.

Three months since you came here, twelve happy weeks. We've loved you and cared for you, and you've given us so much joy in return. All that waiting and wondering, until an unknown teenage girl made the decision to let you go...

Twelve weeks you've been here, but others have waited much, much longer, and now it's our turn to let you go. But you will keep our love, and we will remember you always. Just like all the others we've fostered over the years.

Two cars drew up outside, and Madge took Corinna to the hallway window. Mrs Clancy, the social worker, was in one, and from the other emerged a no-longer-quite-young couple, with pale faces and anxious, excited expressions. The man took an infant car seat from the back of his car and kissed the woman.

Madge wiped her eyes with one hand and smiled at Corinna. 'Come on. Your mum and dad are here. It's time to go home now.'

The Love of My Life

The first time I saw Ellie was at half past four on a Wednesday afternoon in August. By the time we said goodbye, at almost twenty to five, I was realising that I had just met the love of my life. But little did I know that day how much my life would change...

I had a summer job in our local supermarket, stacking shelves and earning enough to keep myself as independently as possible during my final year at uni. The store was one of those huge places that sold everything from garden furniture to caviar, and I was assigned to the non-food section. So on Wednesday afternoon I was tramping round with my scanner, putting in the items that were needed to fill the shelves - and that's when I saw Ellie.

She was wandering down the baby aisle, a small-sized toddler with a pouting lip balanced on one hip, and she obviously wasn't finding what she was looking for. I rushed over to see what I could do. Honestly, it was only then I noticed the gorgeous chocolate-brown hair tumbling over her shoulders, and her big dark eyes, and the beautiful caring expression on her face.

'Dummies!' she announced, before I'd even opened my mouth. 'Please. It's an absolute emergency. I'm looking after Len here while my sister's on holiday and she only left him two dummies – she's trying to wean him off them, actually – but he won't go to sleep without one. The green one should turn up, it's in the house somewhere, but the starry one's vanished – it might be in the sandpit – and it's his favourite.'

'Certainly,' I said briskly, leading her further down the aisle. 'Dummies – here they are, beside the bottles. Any particular kind?'

'Is there a starry one?' she said anxiously. Together we scanned the rows of dummies. 'Yes! Look, Lennie, a lovely new dummy with yellow stars. And here's one with a little sun, too. Let's have two of each, huh?'

She smiled at the baby and then at me, and my heart, which was already going at twice its normal speed, started to thump even more violently. She was just so... she was my home... and she didn't know it.

'That's great,' I said hoarsely. 'I hope he enjoys them. Um... is it fun, looking after him? How old is he?'

'He's fifteen months, and it's amazing,' she said, kissing the baby on both cheeks. 'I love him to bits, but I have to say it's a lot more tiring than my usual holiday job at the snack bar.'

'I'll bet,' I said as we walked slowly towards the check-outs. 'Are you at uni too, then?'

'Teacher training,' she said. 'A year to go. You?'

'Modern languages. I'm Calum Davidson.'

'Ellie Graham.' She stuck out a hand, and my heart nearly exploded at her touch.

'Maybe I'll see you here again, then,' I said, hearing my voice shake. 'I'm here every day this week.' She was second in the queue now...

'Yes,' she said, gazing up at me with those gorgeous eyes. 'See you.'

Slowly, I went back to checking the shelves in the tool aisle, mentally kicking myself for not having asked her out there and then. But maybe she already had a boyfriend – heck, for all I knew she could be married. And I had no idea where she lived or where she was studying. I was going to lose her... On a whim, I dived back to the checkouts, but she was gone.

I would just have to keep an eye open for her.

I watched out so hard over the next couple of days that my eyes began to feel quite gritty, but by Saturday afternoon there had been neither sight nor sound of Ellie and Len. Glumly, I started out on my last section of shelves (men's socks) – and then suddenly there she was, Len in a buggy this time, the starry dummy wedged in his mouth.

'Hi!' said Ellie. 'We were just wondering if you were around, weren't we, Lennie? We're here to get some pasta. Penne for dinner tonight, Len's favourite.'

Len stared up at me in the way that only babies can. Ellie stroked his head, and my heart set off again...

'Great to see you again,' I said, my voice squeaking.

How I wished I could think of something halfway intelligent to say, but my brain had turned to mush.

'Len wanted to show you his dummy, didn't you, lovey?' said Ellie, smiling as the little boy solemnly removed the dummy and waved it at me for a fraction of a second before jamming it very firmly back into his mouth.

I laughed. 'No chance I'll get a go at it, I see.'

She giggled. 'Nope. It's the love of his life.'

I realised I was going to have to do something quickly or she might disappear again, forever this time, and *she* was the love of *my* life.

'Aaah – em – would you like to go for a coffee sometime? Or a meal? Or – anything?'

She looked up at me and grinned, and that was when I knew I would feel this way forever.

'Sounds like a fab idea,' she said.

Relief washed over me. It was like standing in the Indian Ocean on a boiling hot day, and then a wonderful, refreshing, marvellous cool wave comes and splashes over you and it feels like you've gone to heaven...

'Tell you what,' she said, turning the buggy towards the food aisles. 'Why don't we go for a walk in the park tomorrow afternoon? We can feed the ducks and take Len for an ice cream.'

'Brilliant!' I said. We had a date. I would see her again tomorrow. 'Shall we meet at the north gate at half past two?'

Her eyes laughed up at me and I began to have real, agonising hopes that she felt the same way as

I did. Again, I waved goodbye as she went through the checkout, but this time I ran along to the window overlooking the High Street to watch her and Len start off on their walk home. At first there was nothing, then suddenly there they were, on the pavement.

And I knew I was in deep, dark trouble...

Ellie was pushing the buggy with both hands. Wrapped round one hand was a dog lead, and attached to the other end was – well, I wasn't sure what it was. It was huge, and sort of a chestnut brown colour. If I'd seen it in a zoo I'd have said it was a cross between a yak and a bear, with a generous chunk of lion thrown in for good measure.

And I – whisper it – I was really, really scared of dogs.

About eight years ago, I'd had a very unfortunate experience delivering the church magazines for Mum. I won't go into the gory details, but I will say that quite a few people didn't get a mag that month, and I left a nasty confetti-like mess in poor Mrs Whitfield's garden. But then, it was her dog refusing to let me out...

And now I had to face the fact that my darling, wonderful, amazing Ellie had a dog. A huge one. A monster. What on earth was I going to do?

Mum laughed until the tears ran down her cheeks. 'Oh Calum, darling, I'm sorry but you should see your face. Think positive – it might not be Ellie's dog; it might belong to her sister. It sounds like a

Newfoundlander, and they're usually very gentle creatures in spite of their size. And it's high time you did something about this dog-phobia, anyway.'

I googled Newfoundlanders and saw she was right. And as students didn't usually have dogs, it was odds-on that this giant did belong to Ellie's sister. All I had to do was put up a good showing until the sister returned, right? Surely I could do that.

I talked myself into a courageous mood, and by the time I arrived at the north gate the following day I was feeling pretty brave. Quite nonchalant, in fact.

But then a small boy clutching the lead of a marauding spaniel rushed up, and I leapt to one side, my nonchalance deserting me. The boy was followed in quick succession by a family with an extremely energetic labrador, two men with teeth-baring collies and an old lady with one of those vicious Yorkshire terriers.

Then Ellie and Len appeared and, of course, the dog was with them, his lead wound round Ellie's hand again.

'Hi!' she said, smiling up at me. 'This is Max.'

I grabbed Len's buggy before she had the idea of giving me the dog's lead. 'I'll push, shall I?' I realised my voice was two octaves higher than usual, and cleared my throat quickly. 'What shall we do first? You choose.'

Now that was a bad idea if ever I'd had one.

'Let's walk towards the hill,' she said brightly. 'We can let Max off the lead for a run around there, and then we can come back through the rose gardens and on to the play area for an ice cream.'

The very thought of Max 'running around' was enough to bring me out in a cold sweat, but I smiled bravely and nodded as enthusiastically as I could.

We strolled along, Len half-asleep in his buggy, and I have to admit that Max was the picture of placidity, his huge paws plopping along the pathway beside Ellie.

'Is he yours? I asked hopefully, but luck wasn't on my side that day.

'At the moment,' she said. 'He's Mum and Dad's, but they're spending six months in Singapore so I'm looking after him. Laura didn't want to because of Len, you see. It means I have to go home for lunch every day during term-time, but it isn't forever and he's an absolute love, isn't he?'

'Oh – ah – definitely.' I cleared my throat again.

We sat on a bench at the bottom of the hill and talked, Len asleep in his buggy and Max 'running around', which was more like a stroll and a sniff, really. And every single second, I fell deeper and deeper in love. It was incredible. I'd never experienced anything like it. Ellie and I seemed to have the same ideas about all the important things; we were right there on the exact same wavelength. I could see she was looking at me with a pretty gooey expression, too, and I was just about to take her hand, when–

'Woof! Woof!!' Max nosed his way between us, his tail sweeping in front of my nose.

I leapt away – up, I mean – and grabbed the buggy so suddenly that Len was jerked out of his sleep and protested loudly.

'Shall we go on?' I squeaked.

'Max, quiet!' Ellie said, reattaching the lead. She fished around the buggy and produced the starry dummy. 'Here you are, Len-boy. Now, I think Max is probably thirsty, so let's walk on by the pond and then head for the playground. Swings, Lennie!'

On we went, my panic subsiding gradually. But oh, there was no way I could take her hand now, as anyone who has ever gone for a walk with a thirsty Newfoundlander and an energetic toddler in a baby buggy will know. Max seemed to smell the water, and it was all Ellie could do to hold him back to a swift walk.

Things were better when we reached the playground, though. Max lay down for a sleep beside the buggy, and Ellie and I pushed Len on the swings, and then we sat on the little roundabout with him, and we see-sawed and put him down the baby slide. It was fun, but it wasn't earth-shatteringly romantic. We bought ice cream and sat on a bench, but Ellie had both hands full with her own ice and Lennie's. When we'd finished, she cleaned him off with several wet wipes and looked around for a bin.

'I always manage to sit at the other end of the playground to the bin,' she said, laughing, and jogged away with her sticky handful.

Len and I watched her, and I felt quite proud that he was happy being left with me. I was his friend now. I was even allowed to hold the starry dummy while he picked a few choice crumbs from the front of his T-shirt.

That was when it happened. I was watching Ellie as she deposited the wipes in the bin. She was so lovely, surely things would work out for us... I didn't notice the labrador until it was right beside the buggy. Len gave a sudden wail of fright, and Max woke up and leapt to his feet. Before I knew it, I was trapped between two enormous barking dogs and a park bench...

I grabbed Len, fumbling with the strap on the buggy, then stepped up on to the bench and held him well away from the dogs.

'Max! Stop that! Sit!' Ellie's voice rang out.

'Bruno! Quiet! Heel!' The labrador's owner clicked on a lead and turned apologetically to Ellie. 'Sorry about that. He got away before I could grab him.'

'No harm done.' Ellie patted the labrador, who was wagging his tail furiously now – as was Max.

I stepped down from the bench with as much dignity as I could muster, and replaced Len in the buggy. What on earth must Ellie think of me? Leaping up on the bench like that to get away from a couple of soft old dogs... What a coward I was.

We sat in silence for a moment, then Ellie turned to me.

'You're afraid of dogs, aren't you?'

There was no way I could deny it. So I told her about Mrs Whitfield's corgi and the church magazines. She sat and listened, and she didn't laugh.

'Well, I think you were really brave, rescuing Len like that. It must have been awful, getting him out of the buggy between those dogs,' she said.

'I feel like an idiot,' I told her. 'There was no need to panic like that. And oh, Ellie – I really want this to work out – with us, you know.'

She put a hand on my arm and a shiver went right down my spine.

'It will work, don't worry. Let's go home to Laura's. We can stick Max in the kitchen and Len in his sandpit, and drink a nice glass of fizz in the garden, to celebrate finding each other.'

I turned the buggy towards the north gate. 'And when we've done that, can we have a sandcastle competition? I haven't made a sand pie for years.'

She laughed, and put her hand on mine on the buggy. I aimed a kiss at the top of her head and hit exactly the right spot.

'You're on,' she said. 'Hey, we might even find Len's missing dummy!'

'We might,' I said. After all, this was the luckiest day of my life...

A First Time for Everything

The alarm bleeped relentlessly at Brian's side of the bed, and Carla pulled the duvet over her ears as he flung out a hand to switch it off. He yawned as he sat up, and then padded out to the bathroom and turned on the shower.

'Please, oh please Jenny darling, don't wake up.' Carla whispered the words into the warmth of the duvet.

But her plea went unheeded. A thin baby wail came from the cot in the corner, and Carla knew by the tone that her daughter meant business. Time to get up. Again.

She dragged herself out of bed and pulled on her dressing gown, trying to ignore the fuzziness in her head. Her legs felt as if they belonged to someone else, too. She stumbled over to the cot, and immediately, a wonderful feeling of warmth, pride, love and amazement swept through her. Carla lifted Jenny and hugged her tightly, exhaustion forgotten for the moment.

Her baby, hers and Brian's. After all those months

of waiting, they actually had a baby, a beautiful little daughter with dark blue eyes, baby-soft skin, and endearingly downy blonde hair. Carla had never imagined it was possible to feel so much love for one little person. In just five weeks, Jenny had turned their lives upside down, and it was the most wonderful thing that had ever happened to Carla.

If only she wasn't so tired all the time...

Carla changed Jenny, fed her, and took her downstairs where Brian had just finished breakfast. He poured Carla a glass of juice and tickled Jenny's tummy. Jenny waved both arms at him and gurgled solemnly.

'Careful. She's just been fed, and I'm not sure if all the burps are up.' Still holding the baby, Carla sank onto a kitchen chair and sipped her juice.

'Tough night?' Brian was checking through his briefcase.

'Two feeds, and up twice for a cuddle in between times,' said Carla shortly, watching as Brian shrugged into his best-suit jacket and adjusted his tie. He was meeting an important new client this morning.

'Ouch. Poor you. You might catch a nap later, though.' He glanced at her uncertainly.

'A nap's no substitute for a good night's sleep, you must see that.' It was out before she had time to think.

Brian's mouth tightened, and Carla bit her lip. What was happening to them? Five weeks ago, they'd been full of joy, full of pride in themselves and their baby, confident they would cope easily with life as parents. The problem was, thought Carla miserably, she was the one doing all the coping. She was at home all day, being a new mum – exactly what she'd always wanted. But although Brian was as thrilled with Jenny as she was, somehow, he did very little to help, even when he was home. He couldn't breast-feed, of course, but surely he could do some of the walking up and down waiting for the burps? And some of the nocturnal cuddles in between, too? But he ignored the whole uncomfortable up-in-the-night business, and Carla found herself resenting his attitude more and more each day.

'I'm off.' Brian grabbed his briefcase and dropped a kiss on Jenny's head and then on Carla's. 'Carly – it's all right, isn't it? I mean–' He looked at her, eyebrows raised.

'I'm tired, that's all.' Carla only just managed to smile. 'See you tonight.'

Their elderly Ford rattled up the street and round the corner, and Carla took a deep breath.

'Well, chickabiddy, shopping first, then housework, then lunch. And then a lovely long nap, please.'

Jenny blew bubbles at her, and Carla's heart soared. 'I love you so much,' she whispered, cuddling the baby against her cheek and breathing in the warm, sweet baby smell. Why couldn't she and Brian share moments like this with their daughter? But it was the same old story – she was always the one giving the cuddles while Brian looked on. In fact, now she thought about it – he only held Jenny when Carla deposited the baby in his arms.

'Could he possibly be scared he'll drop you?' she said doubtfully. Jenny stared at her seriously. 'Surely not. He's a grown man.'

It was a new idea. Unlike her, Brian had no nieces and nephews. But wouldn't he have said, if he was nervous?

'I'll talk to your dad tonight,' Carla promised, tucking Jenny into the pram. 'If you give us peace for a while, and if I'm still awake by the time he gets home.'

Happier, she went through her planned programme, even managing – joy, oh rapture – a lunchtime nap.

At three o'clock her phone rang.

'Carly!' said Brian excitedly. 'I've sealed the new contract. Mr Johnston was very impressed with our offer and he's sure his firm will do business with us on a permanent basis.' His voice faltered suddenly. 'Thing is, he and his wife live quite near us, and well, I've invited them to dinner. We'll be home well before six, and they won't stay late on a week night. It doesn't need to be anything fancy. Carla?'

Carla's head was reeling. The living room looked like an advertisement for a baby shop, the whole house smelled of baby lotion and sterilising fluid, and none of her posh frocks fitted her again yet. And Jenny was notorious for crying in the evenings. Indignation welled up, but then Carla checked herself. She wasn't just a mum-machine. There should be more to life than coping with her offspring.

'It won't be anything fancy,' she said dryly. 'But I'll

manage.'

'Great,' said Brian. 'Oh, Mrs J's a vegetarian, by the way.'

Carla put her phone down and stood racking her brains. 'Okay,' she said to Jenny. 'We'll have that veggie pasta dish from the freezer, and I'll do guacamole for starters. And ice cream for pud, and we'll buy some of those little ginger waffles to go with it. And cream for the coffee. Come on, Jenny-Penny. Back to the shops.'

She pulled the casserole from the freezer to defrost, dashed to the supermarket and dashed home again, Jenny happily oblivious to the change of routine. Carla laid her down in the living room.

'Watch Mummy do a blitz, now.' She stuffed everything remotely baby-orientated into the big basket, and shoved it into the corner behind the sofa. The dining room was given the same treatment, and Carla began to feel better. The house looked halfway civilised now, as long as their guests didn't start peering behind the furniture. Now – what could she wear? Carla scooped up Jenny and ran upstairs. Mrs Johnston was probably one of those slim, super-elegant young business wives.

Carla searched through her wardrobe and pulled out a below-knee black dress with an elasticated waist. It was ten years old, but it was more or less elegant, and at least she'd be able to breathe in it. She glanced at her watch and panicked.

'I'm never going to be ready!' she wailed, and Jenny looked up at her and wailed right back. It took quarter of an hour to calm the baby, but at last she fell asleep, and Carla laid her in the cot and raced into the shower. She dressed hastily, slapped on a minimum of make-up, and turned her attention to dinner.

Brian and their guests arrived at quarter to six, and Carla was surprised to see that the Johnstons were well into their fifties. She relaxed slightly as Mr Johnston – Martin – immediately began to praise Brian. Carla chatted for a few minutes, then went to see to the dinner while Brian handed out sherry. Sheila Johnston hadn't said much, she thought unhappily. Probably she was wondering how anyone could be such a sloppy housekeeper.

The guacamole, served with tortilla chips and carrot sticks, went down well, however, and Carla watched as Brian and Martin scraped the bowl clean. She stood to gather the plates, and a very determined young voice floated into the room from upstairs.

'You have a baby!' Sheila exclaimed.

Carla felt like crying too. Jenny was going to be crabby for hours now, she could tell. Just cuddle her and sing and walk around, the clinic nurse had said...

Carla grabbed the plates and swept out. 'Yes. I'll just see to her.' She ran upstairs, seized Jenny, who stopped crying in sheer surprise, and rushed back down again. The pasta would burn if she didn't get it out of the oven pronto. Carla plopped Jenny into the baby-seat in the kitchen and turned to the oven.

'Oh, no!' Horrified, she collapsed on a chair and buried her face in her hands. She'd set the oven earlier, and put the pasta dish inside – but she'd forgotten to turn on the heat.

It was the last straw. Carla began to sob helplessly. She was just so damn tired...

'Can I do – Carla, whatever's wrong?' Sheila came in quickly, closing the door behind her.

Carla waved towards the oven, and the older woman's lips twitched. 'Let's turn the heat on, shall we?' She suited the action to the words. 'I did the very same thing the first time we entertained my parents-in-law. Now, you cuddle that gorgeous baby and leave things to me.'

Dazed, Carla watched as Sheila searched around the fridge and cupboards, and speedily produced four bowls of lettuce salad adorned with onion rings and grated cheese, and a garlicky sauce.

She winked at Carla. 'Come on. And not a word about the oven. Just eat slowly and keep the conversation going. They'll never guess.'

And although Brian looked puzzled, Martin was loud in his praise of the second starter. Conversation centred round Jenny, who settled down in Sheila's arms, and for the first time that day Carla felt calm. At last, someone was helping her.

After that, the evening was a success. Carla took Jenny upstairs to bed after coffee, and returned to find Sheila loading the dishwasher.

'Brian and Martin are deep in business talk. So here I am. You look tired, love. Babies are exhausting. Do you have family nearby to help out?'

Carla shook her head. 'Brian's folks are dead, and my family all live in Wales. I do get tired – but we manage.'

'Brian was very naughty to invite us at such short notice,' said Sheila. 'Carla, if you ever need a substitute grandma, give me a ring. I'd love to babysit for a few hours and let you go to the hairdresser or whatever.'

'Or have a sleep!' Carla smiled shakily. 'I'll take you up on that!'

She and Brian waved as their new friends drove home a little later.

'That was great. Thanks, love.' Brian pulled Carla close, and she felt him stiffen as Jenny's voice sounded upstairs.

'Bri – why don't you like lifting her?'

He looked uncomfortable. 'I'm no good with babies. I don't know how to hold her or–'

Carla pushed him towards the stairs. 'Nonsense. Go and give her a cuddle and see if she'll settle. Go on – she won't bite you.'

After a moment there was silence upstairs. Carla sat on the sofa, exhausted. Had she done the right thing, pushing Brian like that? But he had to learn – Jenny was his daughter too.

She was half-asleep when Brian crept back into the room, the baby in his arms. 'Carly – look! I had the first one all to myself, but maybe she'll do it again.

Come on, Jenny, show Mummy!' he said excitedly, and Carla stared.

Jenny looked up at her, and a real, definite, wonderful baby smile spread over the little face.

'Oh! Her first smile!' Weariness flew out of the window, and Carla hugged them both.

'Her second one,' said Brian smugly, his own face one big beam.

Carla giggled at the pride in his voice. Clever Jenny, producing that first smile just when Brian needed a confidence booster. And now it had started, the daddy and daughter bonding would continue. They were a family at last – and it felt good!

Lucky for Some

I was furious with Phil. I grabbed the car key from the hall table and shrugged into my jacket. I'd been right in the middle of a tricky bit in my essay – and it was going really well, too – when my twin brother, an enthusiastic member of the local bike club, phoned to say he'd biked into a hole and done something dreadful to his front wheel. Would I pick him up? It was a long way to walk home, carrying an injured bike.

I stomped outside, then drove Dad's car the four miles to Wethermere Cycling Club's headquarters, a dilapidated wooden cabin by the lake. Phil and a couple of others were standing around outside.

'If I can't get back into that essay, I'll strangle you,' I said grimly, helping him hoist his bike to the roof rack.

Phil grinned. He had a very fetching grin, probably the main reason he always had a string of girlfriends wandering after him. 'Thank you a hundred thousand times,' he said. 'Don't be cross. I'll fix the house up for Mum and Dad coming back, and you can get on with your essay.'

Our parents had spent the last two weeks sunning themselves in the south of Italy. Phil and I had arranged to be home by five to make the place look a bit more civilised for them coming home tomorrow.

I sniffed. 'Okay.'

Phil lowered himself into the passenger seat, and I was just fastening my seat belt when a figure came out of the clubhouse. I blinked, twice. This was Prince Charming personified. He was everything a girl could wish for. Tall, dark – well, more golden-brown, actually – but definitely handsome. He exchanged a few words with the bikers still hanging around, waved to Phil, glanced at me, then swung his leg over his bike and pedalled off, leaving me with a very odd feeling in the pit of my stomach. Suddenly, I knew this was an absolutely important moment in my life.

I became aware that Phil was chortling quietly beside me.

'Handsome Harry Carstairs,' he said. 'Aged twenty-three, IT technician at Wethermere Health Board, own flat, own car, lots of interested females but, as yet, unattached... shall I go on?'

I slammed the car into gear and exited the car park, feeling very foolish. 'Why should I be interested?' I said, sticking my nose in the air. But he knew me too well.

'Come off it. Your chin nearly hit your chest when you saw him. He's a nice bloke, actually.'

I sniffed again, and we drove home in silence.

Back at my laptop, I gave myself a good talking

to. 'You're a daft brush, Hilary Becket, letting one glimpse of a good-looking bloke turn your head like that. Forget him. Concentrate on your exams.'

I was studying Psychology, Sociology and Economics, and had a job with the housing association all lined up for September, when my course finished. I'd had boyfriends, of course, but no one special, and to be honest, I was beginning to feel rather single. Two of my school friends were married already, and nearly everyone had a steady boyfriend. I sighed. My finals were looming, so I took my own advice and (almost) forgot about Harry for the next few weeks.

I might have (almost) forgotten about him for longer, if the bike club hadn't organised a 'Cross-Country for Everyone' event, to raise money for a new clubhouse roof.

'Just the thing for lazy bikers like you, Hilary,' said Phil, one Sunday morning at breakfast time. 'We're marking out two courses – five miles for kids and ten miles for adults, with a prize for the quickest round on each course. There's a refreshment stand at the halfway point on each, and...' He smirked at me. 'Handsome Harry's manning the ten-mile one.'

'Who's Handsome Harry?' Mum asked, refilling coffee cups all round.

'Hil's latest heart-throb,' he said mockingly. 'I know, I know – you're past the heart-throb stage. But I'll bet you a dinner for two at Alphonso's that you don't get round the ten-mile course.'

'Start saving!' I retorted, and he laughed knowingly.

Dad helped me fix up my bike that weekend. It wasn't exactly the latest model, but I reckoned it would get me round the course. I started training – I hadn't biked seriously for years – and by the end of two weeks I was quietly confident I would manage ten miles with elegance and ease. Not that all this had anything to do with impressing Harry, of course.

I sent in my entrance fee, and Phil brought home my number. It was 13.

'So who's superstitious?' I said to Phil, trying on my new helmet. It was going to be difficult to look glamorous and interesting with a thing like that on my head...

'Shall I tell Harry to watch out for you?' My brother pretended to look concerned.

'Of course not. I'd forgotten all about him,' I lied.

The morning of the rally dawned cloudless and mild, just right for biking. Phil and I drove to the start and parted company – he was timing the five milers. I joined the ten-mile people at the other end of the car park.

Number 14 was Joe Preston, an old school friend who worked at the bank. 12 was Alice Morton, one of Phil's numerous girlfriends.

She grinned at me. 'So Phil roped you in too? He promised to take me to dinner at Alphonso's if I got round. I couldn't resist!'

I smiled grimly. This rally was going to cost Phil a packet. Off we set, one minute apart. I enjoyed the first part of the course. The countryside was glorious, and the air smelled fresh and clean. Joe Preston caught up with me fairly quickly and we biked along together, chatting about our old school class.

We were just coming up to the halfway mark – not that I was looking out for it, of course – when things started to go wrong.

Alice, some yards in front of Joe and me, suddenly did a terrific wobble and swayed about all over the track. We were going downhill, and in less time than it takes to say it, Joe and I were on top of her. We all braked frantically, then fell over each other into an extremely muddy ditch, right opposite the refreshments stand.

Joe jumped up and hauled me to my feet. 'All right?' He fussed around, wiping mud from my face and helmet and rescuing my bike. I was aware that Harry had rushed over and was helping Alice, who had, somehow, managed to get hardly muddy at all.

'Sorry, you two,' she said. 'I hit a stone, and – well, I was daydreaming. You know the rest...' She laughed merrily, and Harry laughed too. He led her over to the stand and presented her with a plastic cup of juice. They stood there, heads together, talking quietly.

Joe fetched me some juice, too. 'Are you okay to go on?'

I nodded glumly. At least I could get that dinner at Alphonso's out of Phil...

That evening I lay soaking in a hot bath, and vowed never, ever to let my brother persuade me into doing anything like that again. Mind you, it had been fun until we landed in the ditch. And even then, the only thing that was hurt was my pride. Harry hadn't given me a second look as he'd rushed over to help Alice. Of course, Joe was already helping me. Maybe there was something in the unlucky 13 superstition after all...

The next day, I poured my heart out to Mum. She smiled at me very gently.

'You're tired, chick. You've worked hard all year and you've done well. Things'll look different in a few months when you've started your job and found a nice flat. Anyway, what makes you think you need a life-partner to be happy, at your age? Have fun! I was twenty-nine before I met your dad.'

Wise words, and I recognised their truth. You're being juvenile, Hilary Becket, I scolded myself. So I did my best to forget Harry. Again.

And of course, Mum's words of wisdom came true. Life took on quite a different hue when I'd started my job and found a flat to share with a friend from uni. I was my own mistress now, and I found that the presence or absence of a boyfriend had little to do with being happy and fulfilled. I even went out a few times with Joe from the bank, and we had good fun reminiscing about primary school. Harry seemed to have disappeared off the face of the earth, though I have to admit I didn't go anywhere near the bike club.

Then Mum fell and sprained her wrist, so I went back home for a week to help her out. Dad was hopeless in the kitchen, and Phil had his own flat now, too.

'It's the Guild Bazaar on Saturday afternoon, love,' said Mum on Thursday evening. 'I was supposed to be helping with the teas.'

'I'll do it,' I said promptly. The home-baking at Guild Bazaars was second to none. I glanced at the calendar and realised that Saturday was the thirteenth. Oh, well – at least it wasn't a Friday.

Mrs Bainbridge, the president of the Bazaar Committee, gave me the job of keeping a supply of cakes and scones on the buffet table, and I spent the next hour running to the kitchen with empty plates and returning with full ones. Lots of Mum's friends were there, and I had to explain, at least ten times, what I was up to nowadays. After a bit there was a lull, and I actually stood still for a moment and looked around the hall. Most of the tables were occupied, and a buzz of conversation filled the air.

Suddenly, something hit me from behind – hard. To my horror, I found myself face down on the floor, completely winded.

'Oh no – I'm so sorry! Trust me, I knew I should have waited in the car, but my mother persuaded me to come in. Are you okay?'

A man's voice spoke above me, and two hands hoisted me to my feet again. I turned round and nearly fainted. It was Handsome Harry. He brushed a few specks of dust from my shoulder as Mrs Bainbridge bustled up.

'Hilary, what a nasty tumble.' She treated Harry to a very hard stare. 'Take a break, dear, and have a cup of tea.'

Harry gripped my elbow and led me to an empty table. He fetched me a cup of tea and a piece of caramel shortbread, and sat down opposite with his own rations. Suddenly he grinned.

'You were number 13 in the bike race and landed in the ditch, and now it's the 13th and I knocked you off your feet. It's not your lucky number, is it?'

My heart gave a huge thump and raced off. He'd remembered my number...

I smiled sweetly. 'That's no reason to flatten me on church premises just for the pleasure of having afternoon tea with me.' These days, I was a whole lot more savvy about talking to attractive men.

Harry laughed. 'Let's not leave it at a cup of bazaar tea. We could have dinner sometime – please? Alphonso's in town is really good.'

I pondered. Dinner with Harry might be the start of something big, or it might not. Either way, I was an independent person now. All at once I remembered something, and beamed at Harry.

'Dinner at Alphonso's would be lovely,' I said. 'Thank you. But we'll send the bill to my brother – I've just remembered a debt he hasn't paid.'

Harry smiled and nodded, though he looked puzzled, as well he might. Suddenly I felt very, very happy. This *was* the start of something big; I could tell. Maybe 13 was my lucky number after all...

The Saturday Secret

Isobel Adams carried her coffee outside to the wooden seat by the roses. Life was good, she decided, watching two sparrows flutter in a sunny pool of water left by yesterday's rain. Young Jake was quite independent now, so she and Eric had more time to themselves than they'd had in years. And Sally was about to make her a grandmother. Yes, she could be proud of her children, and now that Mum was safely installed in the granny flat, there was nothing left to worry about.

'Hi there!' Fourteen-year-old Jake strode up the path and flopped down beside Isobel.

'You're back early. Good game?'

'Nope. We lost five-nil,' said Jake cheerfully.

Isobel laughed. Jake's terrible football team was the family joke.

A car turned into the driveway and lurched to a stop behind Eric's Fiat. Isobel's daughter, heavily pregnant, extracted herself from the driver's seat and waddled over to sit on Isobel's other side. 'Hello, you two. Mind if I invite myself to stay the night? Fred has a darts tournament.'

'That would be lovely, darling!' Isobel felt a surge of pleasure. The family would all be under one roof tonight – it didn't often happen now.

'I've been meaning to ask – what on earth was Gran up to last Saturday?' Sally nodded towards the granny flat at the side of the house.

'Up to?' Isobel stared.

'I saw her in town at eleven o'clock, standing at the bus stop in the pouring rain.'

Isobel shrugged. Saturday had been wet from dawn to dusk. Surely there had been no need for Gran to go into town on a day like that? But then, her mother was fiercely independent and more than capable of leading her own life.

'I've seen her go out at quarter to eight the past three or four Saturday mornings,' said Jake. 'You know, when I get up early for footie training. She never did that, before.'

Isobel was astounded. 'Quarter to… She used to snooze until ten on a Saturday! Why didn't you say?'

'Well, it's up to Gran, isn't it?' said Jake. 'She can do what she likes.'

Isobel glared at the roses, her complacent mood gone. Jake was right. Her mother could – and would – do as she liked, and as the granny flat had its own front door she was disturbing no one with her early-morning jaunts.

'The mystery woman!' said Sally, giggling. 'She must want to keep it a secret or she'd have told us about – whatever it is.'

'I wish I knew...' Isobel bit her lip.

'Curiosity killed the cat, Mum,' said Sally. 'Maybe she's taken up sketching. Or ballroom dancing.'

Jake spluttered. 'Or maybe she's learning the trumpet, or–'

Isobel couldn't help laughing. 'Oh, don't be daft! How could she be learning the trumpet – we'd have noticed!'

Sally took the wind right out of her sails. 'Maybe she has a man-friend.'

Isobel struggled to keep her mouth closed. The idea had never entered her head, but after all – why not? Her mother was an attractive woman.

'At quarter to eight in the morning?' she said weakly.

Sally pushed herself to her feet. 'Breakfast in town, followed by – dancing, or painting, or whatever.'

The next day, Isobel confided her newly-found worries to her husband. Much to her indignation, Eric laughed heartily.

'Good for Gran! Whatever she's up to, she's leading her own life, just like you wanted her to. If she was still in Dunvegan Road we wouldn't have known a thing about it.'

It was true, thought Isobel. The granny flat was a convenience and not a necessity, built when her mother had been forced to sell her house to make way for the new ring road. But... Gran had such a bubbly, out-going personality – usually she was the first person to rush home and tell the whole family about her various doings. All this secrecy seemed very out of character. Isobel decided to do a little careful prodding.

On Friday morning, she knocked on the granny flat door. 'Come into town with me tomorrow morning, Mum? I'd like your help finding a posh frock for Sue's anniversary party.'

'Sorry, dear, I've, um, arranged something else for tomorrow,' said her mother firmly. 'Let's go this afternoon. You've nothing special on, have you?'

Isobel could only agree. And despite several loaded questions, she returned home none the wiser about what Gran was doing the following day. And even after the afternoon's three-hour shopping expedition, she still didn't know!

'Could it possibly be a – a date? With a man, I mean? I hope she knows what she's doing!'

Jake grinned across the dinner table. 'I bet she worried about your dates often enough! The tables are turned now, aren't they?'

Isobel glared, and he reached out and patted her shoulder. 'Don't worry, Mum. I'll leave early for training tomorrow, and bump into Gran in the garden. She'll have to say something about what she's up to.'

Peeking out from behind her bedroom curtains early the next morning, Isobel watched as Jake carried out his plan. There was her mother, promptly at quarter to eight... and Jake, sports bag in one hand, a piece of toast in the other. They had a brief conversation at the garden gate, then strode off in opposite directions.

Saturday morning had never seemed so long, but at last Jake arrived home for lunch. Isobel followed him upstairs.

'Well? What did she say? Where was she going?'

Jake shrugged. 'She said, 'Morning Jake, off to training?' I said, 'Yup, home game this afternoon, where are you off to?' And she said—'

'What? What did she say?'

'Wayland Road,' said Jake, and Isobel groaned. Wayland Road stretched right across town and was the main shopping street. Dancing, trumpet lessons, sketching – anything was possible on Wayland Road.

'Sorry,' said Jake.

Isobel gave up. Her mother was obviously happy having her Saturday secret. There didn't seem much they could do about it.

The following Thursday, Sally phoned. 'Oh Mum!' she wailed, and Isobel's heart immediately rushed into top gear. Was it the baby?

'No, no,' said Sally. 'It's Fred. You know his darts team made it to the Championship final? Well, it's this weekend – in Edinburgh – and he's going!'

'Oh, dear,' said Isobel helplessly, and really, it did seem thoughtless of Fred to go so far with the baby due next week. 'Couldn't he ask someone to replace him?'

'They've all got this flu bug that's going round,' said Sally. 'If he doesn't go, they can't make up a team. I suppose I'm silly to get into a state about it.'

'You're not, darling, but remember what they say

– first babies...'

'...are always late!' They finished together, and Sally managed a weak giggle.

'Thanks, Mum. You always keep things in perspective. I can come for another night or two, can't I?'

Isobel chatted for a few minutes and then rang off, smiling. Being a mum didn't stop when your children flew the nest and became parents themselves, and what a good feeling that was.

That evening, Eric came home from work with a strange expression on his face. 'Have you found out what Gran's been up to, with her 'dates'?'

Isobel looked up from the pie she was about to push into the oven. 'Only that they seem to be regular on Saturday mornings. Why?'

Eric sat down at the kitchen table. 'I noticed some broken glass in the gutter when I turned into the driveway, so I went back to lift it. Gran was just coming out of Jeff McLean's house; they were both standing in the front porch. She seemed very excited, kissed him on both cheeks, and then he gave her what looked like a bottle of champagne, and then – well, I didn't want to be caught spying on them, so I came inside.'

Isobel gaped at him. Jeff McLean, the neighbour across the road, was a confirmed bachelor and at least fifteen years younger than Gran.

'They can't be – do you think – oh, Eric! But I know – I'll invite her over for coffee tonight.' Isobel rushed for her jacket.

Gran's cheeks were suspiciously pink when she opened the door. 'Thank you, dear – that would be lovely.'

Isobel hesitated. 'Did you have a good day?' she ventured at last, and her mother gave a little snigger.

'I had a brill day, as Jake would say, and I'll tell you about it on Saturday. You're all invited to dinner. No – not another word!'

Isobel trailed home. 'At least we'll know on Saturday,' she said to Eric. 'Oh, dear, do you think–'

'Exciting, huh?'

Isobel gave him a look. It was a bit too exciting for her taste.

Saturday morning dawned cold and blustery. Jake went off to his football training as usual, but as far as Isobel could see there was no movement in the granny-flat. At ten o'clock Sally arrived.

'That's a real gale out there. They're making lorries go over the bridge in twos.' She eased herself into the sofa and sat clutching her bump. 'Golly, what was that?'

A plastic bin had blown right across the garden. Eric went to deal with it.

'You won't believe this, but Gran's been out,' he said when he came back. 'I've just seen her go back into her flat, all dressed up in her new pants suit, and she didn't half look pleased with herself.'

'Alone?' Isobel and Sally spoke together, and Eric nodded.

Jake's football match was cancelled, so he and Eric

went off to the sports centre for a swim while Isobel and Sally sat looking through some old photo albums. The gale increased, and then the rain started, huge drops that battered against the windows and turned the front path into a miniature stream.

Isobel felt very apprehensive. She was worried about her mother, and now she was worried about Sally too. Her daughter was pale and obviously not comfortable, though she insisted that everything was all right.

At three o'clock Gran appeared to borrow Isobel's hand mixer, and stayed for coffee. Isobel squinted at her mother in the opposite chair, but Gran appeared to be her usual self – no unduly pink cheeks today, though her eyes were twinkling brightly. Isobel sighed. They'd hear about the secret in Gran's good time. She was about to suggest a round of gin rummy when Sally gave a low moan.

'Mum – Gran – oh Mum, I think the baby's coming!'

Isobel rushed to the girl's side. 'Deep breaths, darling. Don't worry; it's probably a false alarm.'

Sally breathed obediently, then groaned again. 'It's coming, Mum! I have to get to the hospital–'

Isobel had a brief moment of panic. Eric had taken the car. They would have to phone for an ambulance, or maybe a neighbour could drive them...

Gran stood up, an indescribable expression on her face. 'Isobel, help Sally into her coat.' She sounded unbelievably calm and just a little triumphant. 'I'll drive you.'

Isobel's mouth fell open. 'But you can't drive!'

'Oh yes, I can.' Gran was pulling on her own jacket. 'I've had lessons every Saturday for the past six months. I passed my test on Thursday, and Jeff McLean across the road has sold me his car. I collected the keys this morning. Come on, there's no time to lose!'

Sally managed a weak giggle. 'We thought it was – trumpet lessons!'

Isobel smiled in spite of herself. Trust her mother to do the unexpected!

An hour and fifty minutes later, baby Emily blinked in the bright lights of the delivery room.

'Sally, she's gorgeous!' Isobel's eyes were full of tears. 'Well done, darling!'

'And well done, Gran!' Sally looked across at her grandmother. 'But why all the secrecy?'

'I wanted to surprise you. I thought a car would be useful for going places – make me more independent. I didn't think my first drive as a non-learner would be quite so dramatic!'

Isobel squeezed her mother's hand. 'I hope I'm as super when I'm your age!'

Sally kissed the baby's head and grinned at her grandmother. 'Super-gran, that's you. 'No – you're Super-great-gran now, aren't you?'

Gran had never looked more proud. 'Super-great-gran,' she agreed happily. 'On wheels!'

If you enjoyed these stories, why not try one of Melinda Huber's novellas?

A Lake in Switzerland

Stacy can't believe her luck when her best friend Emily invites her on a holiday to Switzerland.

She arrives at the Lakeside Hotel with high hopes, but the problems begin straightaway. Emily's recent injury doesn't let her do much, and something is wrong at the hotel. Where are all the guests? Why is the owner's son so bad-tempered? And then there's the odd behaviour of Stacy's fiancé, back home. It's hard to enjoy the scenery with all this going on...

By the last day of the holiday, Stacy knows her life will never be the same again – but the end of the week is just the beginning of the Lakeside adventure.

Also available from Fabrian Books

Daffodil Days: Stories from the
Broome Park Prefab Village
by Pat Posner

Welcome to Broome Park Prefab Village!

Step back in time to the early 1950s when the aftermath of World War Two was still etched deeply in memories, some foods were still on ration, menfolk were on – or returning from – National Service and Britain was about to crown a new queen.

This collection of stories is about the families who live in Broome Park Prefab Village. Stories of friendship, good neighbours, a war widow whose young daughter wishes for a Daddy, love and romance, a very special Christmas, shared problems and the occasional crime.

Cobblestone Cove: A collection of short stories
By Zara Thorne

This is a collection of thirteen short stories, most of which were previously published in The People's Friend magazine under the author's real name, Deirdre Palmer.

The characters you will meet are of all ages and backgrounds, each with their own way of seeing the world and dealing with its dilemmas.

Take a trip back in time to the 1930s when fourteen-year-old Stella agonises over her first love, and to the 1960s when single mum Lizzie comes face-to-face with her past on a Bank Holiday trip to Brighton.

Back in the present day, young Molly finds the strength to face her problems in, of all places, a garden centre. It takes a trip to the Troodos mountains in Cyprus to restore Carl's faith in life; Paloma finds the path to her future in a seaside village in Devon, while the residents of exclusive Ivory Park are dismayed to find that high walls and security gates are no protection against crime.

Coffee-break, commute, beach or fireside – your quick read is here. Dip in and enjoy.

About the Author

Linda Huber grew up in Glasgow, Scotland, but went to work in Switzerland for a year aged twenty-two, and has lived there ever since. Her day jobs have included working as a physiotherapist in hospitals and schools for handicapped children, and teaching English in a medieval castle. Not to mention several years as a full-time mum to two boys and a rescue dog.

Linda's writing career began in the nineties, and since then she's had over fifty short stories and articles published, as well as five psychological suspense novels. Her books are set in places she knows well – Cornwall (childhood holidays), The Isle of Arran (teenage summers), Yorkshire (visiting family), as well as Bedford and Manchester (visiting friends).

Her latest project is a series of feel-good novellas set in Switzerland. *A Lake in Switzerland, A Spa in Switzerland*, and *Trouble in Switzerland* will all be published in 2018 under her feel-good pen name Melinda Huber.

Find out more about Linda here: viewAuthor.at/LindaHuber or follow her blog for details of new releases and life in lovely Switzerland. https://lindahuber.net/blog/